PETER PLA

BOG

AGAIN

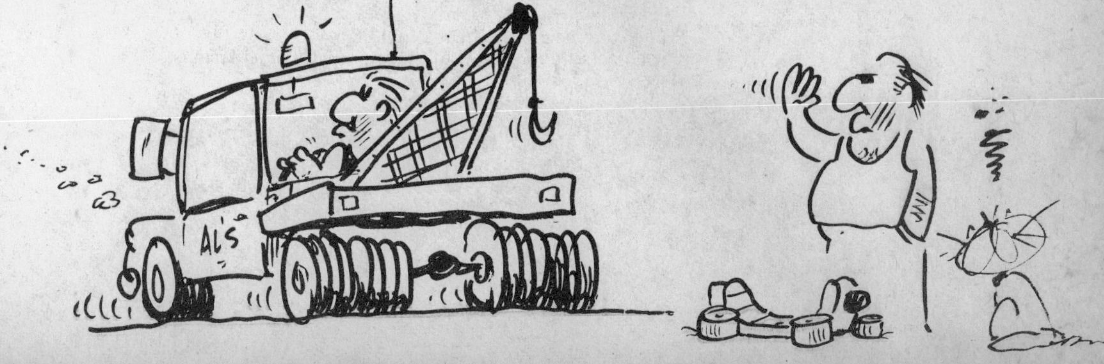

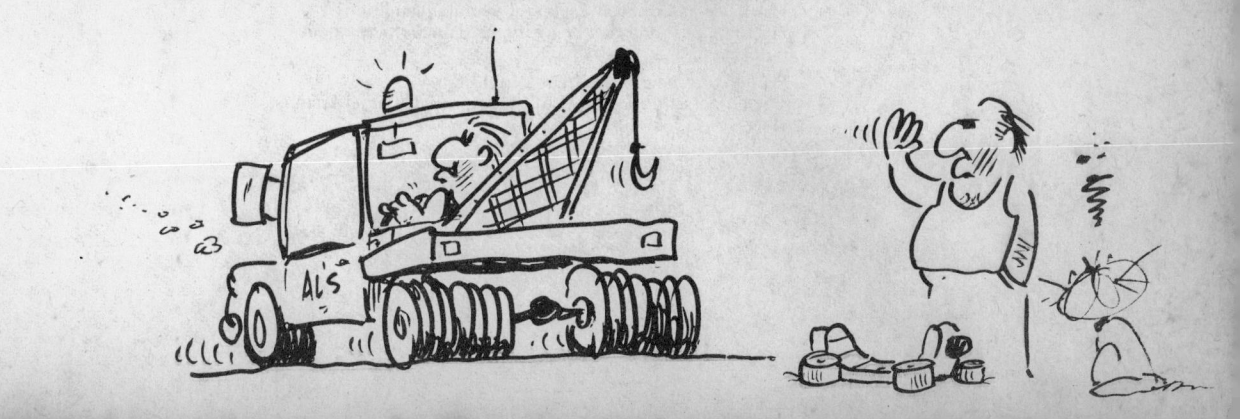

Arrow Books Limited
62-65 Chandos Place, London WC2N 4NW

An imprint of Century Hutchinson Limited

London Melbourne Sydney Auckland
Johannesburg and agencies throughout
the world

First published 1986

Bogart appears daily in *Today*

©Peter Plant 1986

This book is sold subject to the condition that it shall not, by way of trade or otherwise, be lent, resold, hired out, or otherwise circulated without the publisher's prior consent in any form of binding or cover other than that in which it is published and without a similar condition including this condition being imposed on the subsequent purchaser

Printed and bound in Great Britain by
The Guernsey Press Co. Ltd., Guernsey, Channel Islands.

ISBN 0 09 946240 0

BOGART'S GIRLFRIEND, MANDY, TALKS ABOUT BOGART:

❝ MAKING THIS BOOK PUT A TREMENDOUS STRAIN ON OUR RELATIONSHIP. HE INSISTED ON DOING HIS OWN STUNTS AND, WELL, HE DID ALL THE LOVE SCENES 'FOR REAL'. ONE EVENING HE DID FORTY-SEVEN 'TAKES' BEFORE HE WAS SATISFIED IT WAS RIGHT. HE PUSHED HIMSELF, AND THE CAST, CONSTANTLY. ONE DAY, WHEN HE FOUND OUT PETER, HIS CARTOONIST, HAD ALLOWED A 'SOFT' GAG TO GET THROUGH, HE WENT BERSERK. I THINK THAT'S THE ONLY TIME I EVER SAW BOGART LOSE HIS TEMPER. THEN, WHEN IT WAS ALL FINISHED, AND OVER AT THE PUBLISHERS, HE TOOK EVERYONE OUT TO ANDY'S FOR FISH AND CHIPS! SO TYPICAL! I HOPE THERE ISN'T GOING TO BE A THIRD BOOK. ❞

A LOT IS SAID ABOUT CATS...
SOME PEOPLE SAY WE'RE WARM AND AFFECTIONATE...
BOOT!
WHAZZZ

SOME SAY WE'RE CUNNING AND CLEVER...
RRRRRRRR
BAM
YELP!
SOME SAY SYMPATHETIC AND KIND...

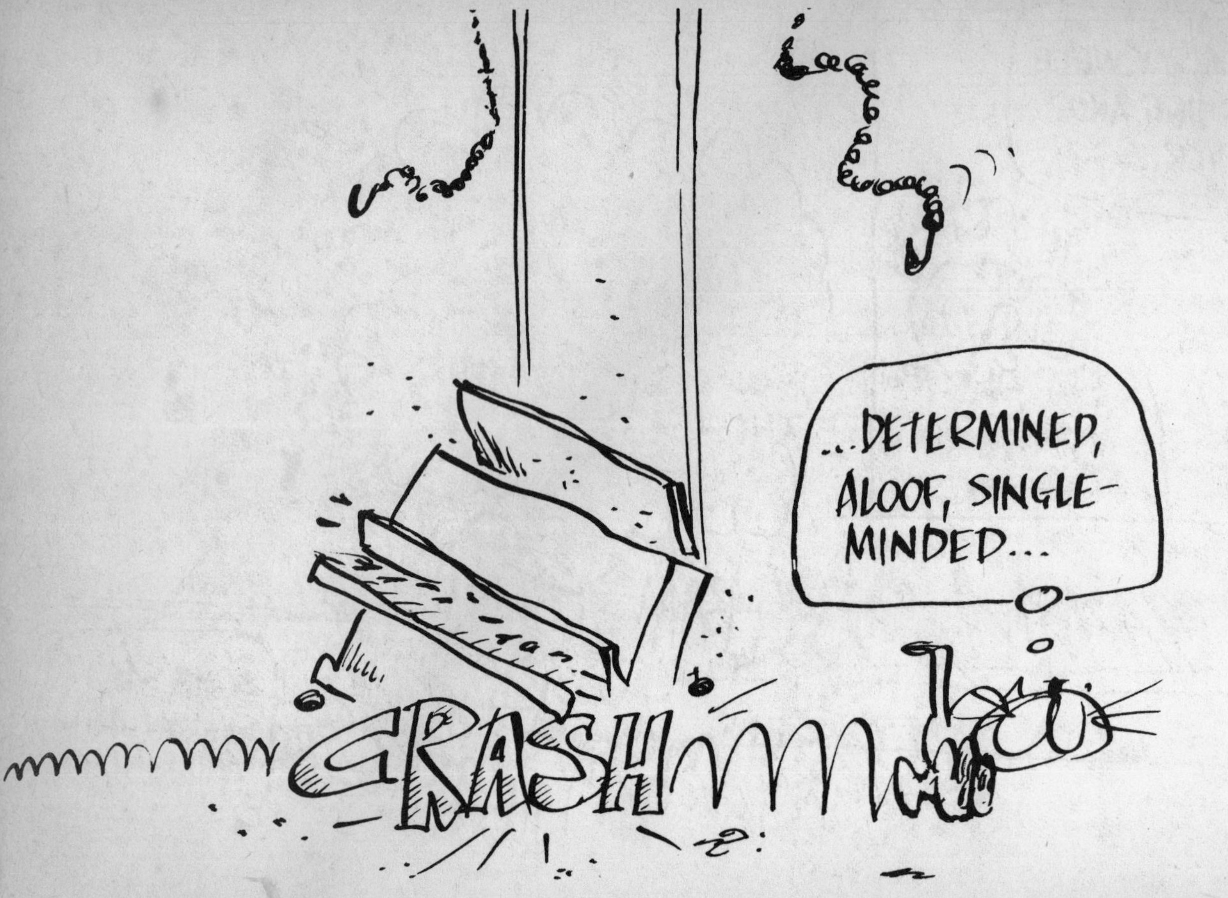
...DETERMINED, ALOOF, SINGLE-MINDED...
CRASH

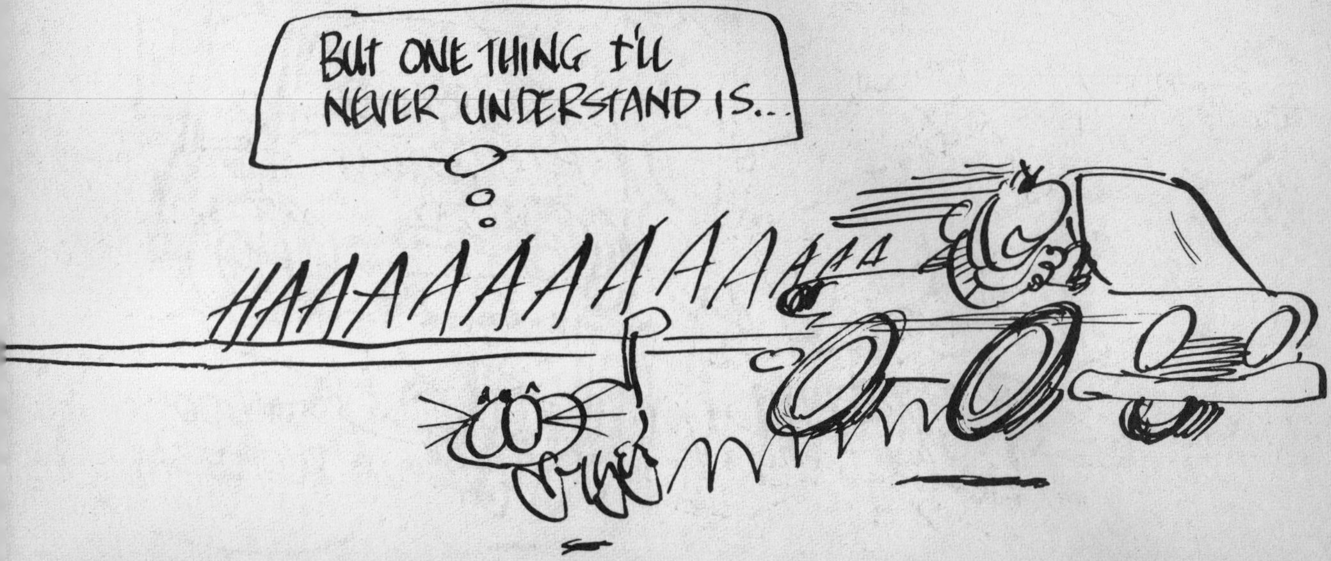
BUT ONE THING I'LL NEVER UNDERSTAND IS...
HAAAAAAAAAAAAA

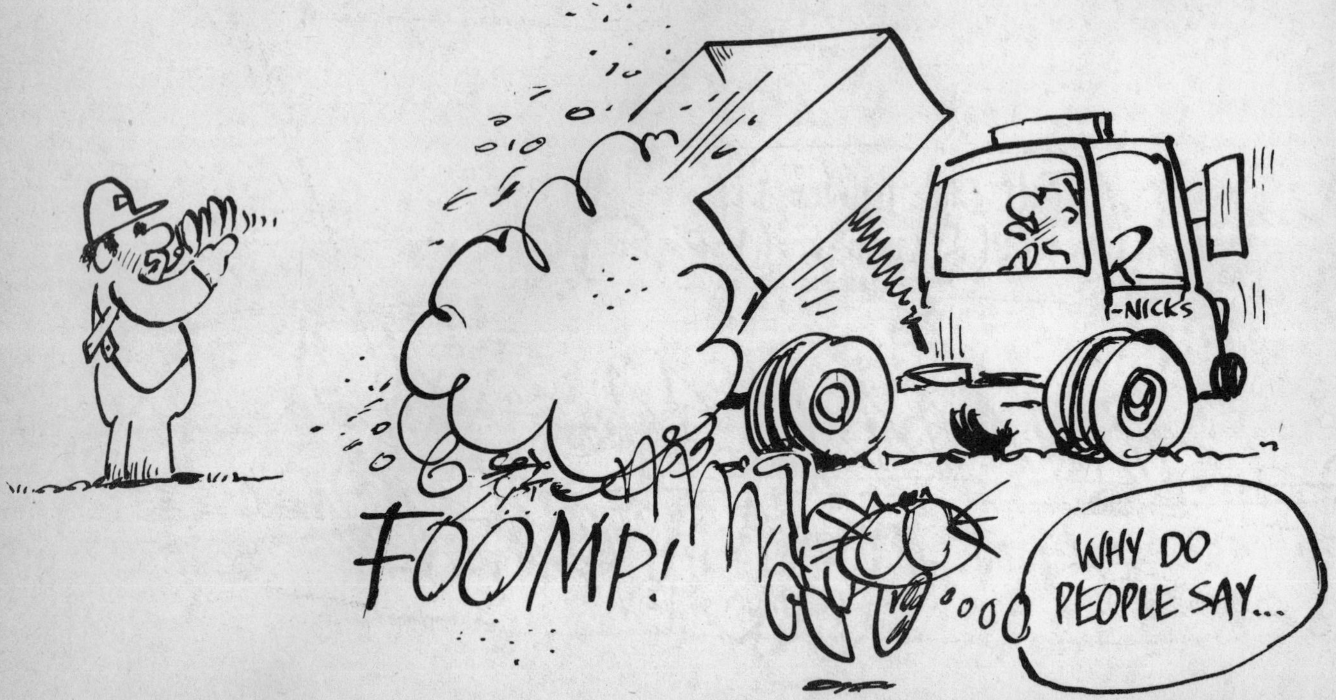

NICKS
FOOMP!
WHY DO PEOPLE SAY...

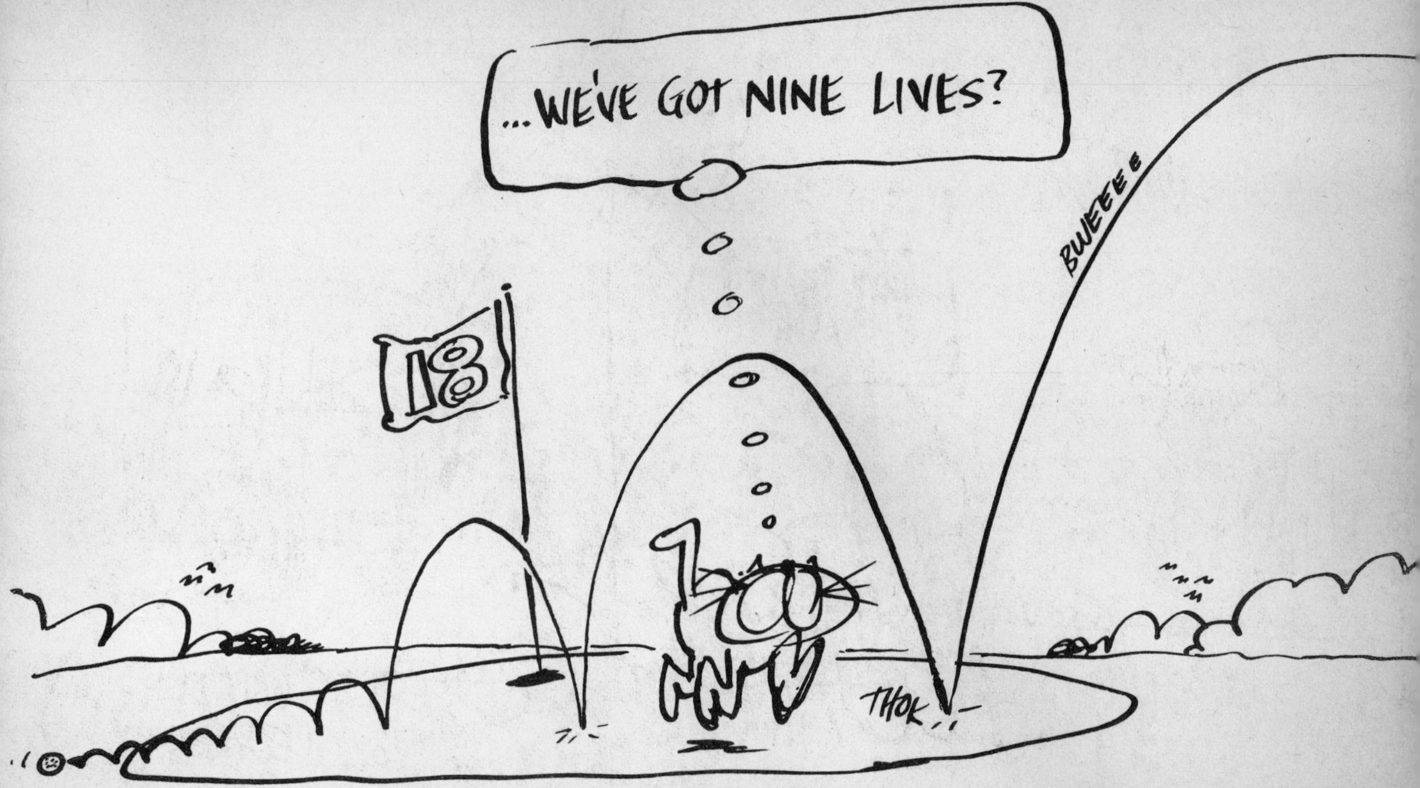

...WE'VE GOT NINE LIVES?
18
BWEEEE
THOK

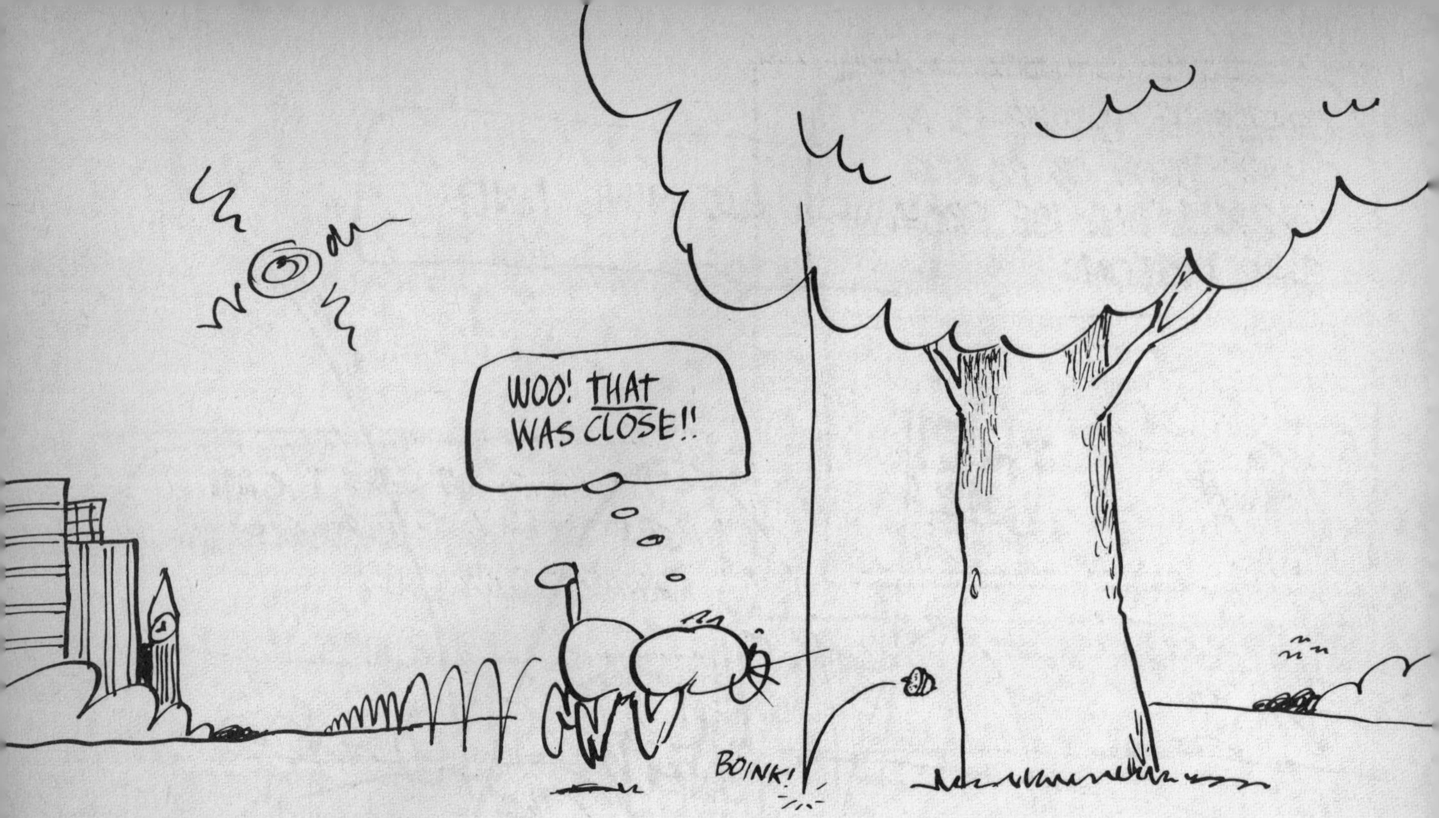
WOO! THAT WAS CLOSE!!
BOINK!

OBSERVE. THERE IS A THICK PANE OF GLASS SEPARATING ME FROM THIS PIGEON.

THERE IS NO WAY I CAN GET TO HIM. THE PIGEON IS COMPLETELY SAFE.

TAP
TAP
AWK!
BUT THAT DOESN'T MAKE ANY DIFFERENCE TO THE PIGEON.
FLAP
FLAP
FLAP
FLAP

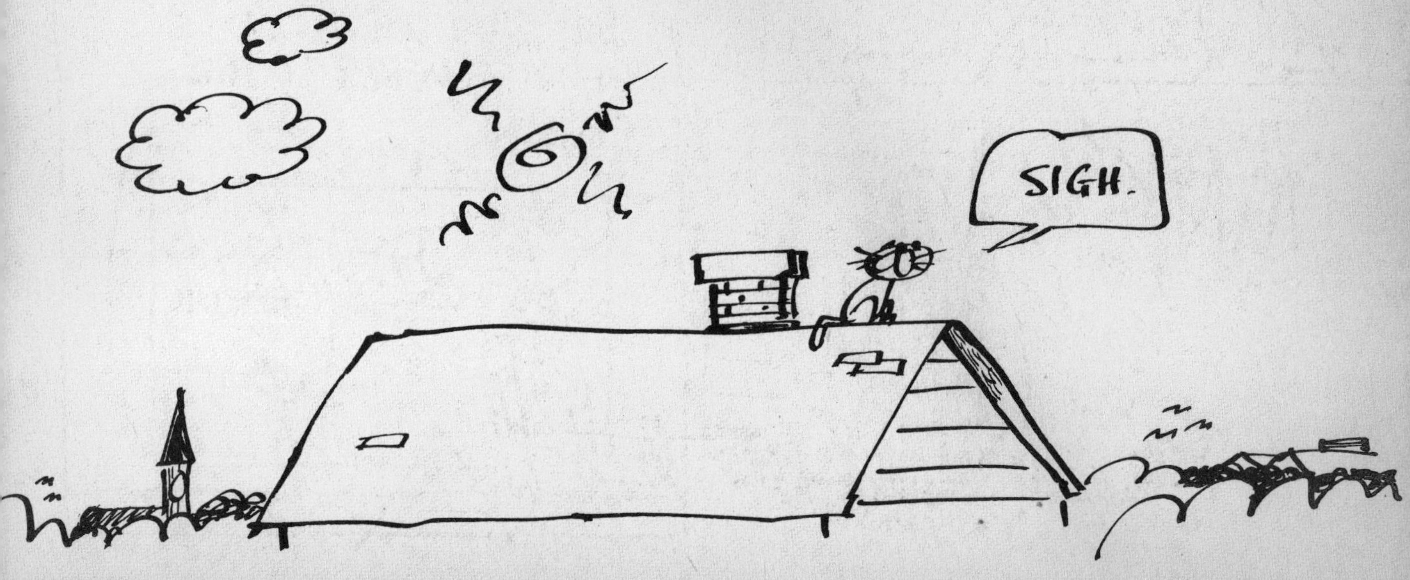
SIGH.

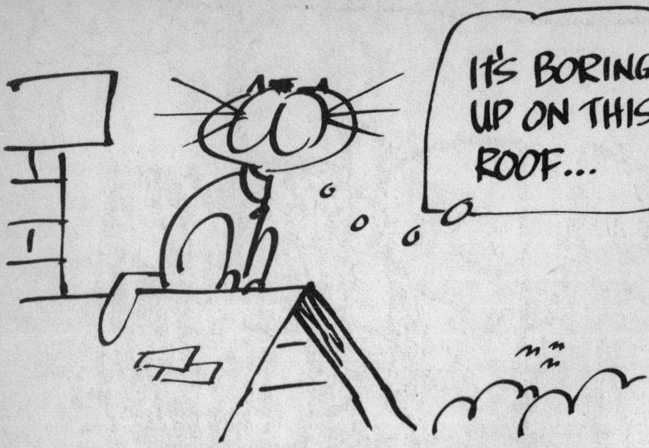
IT'S BORING UP ON THIS ROOF...

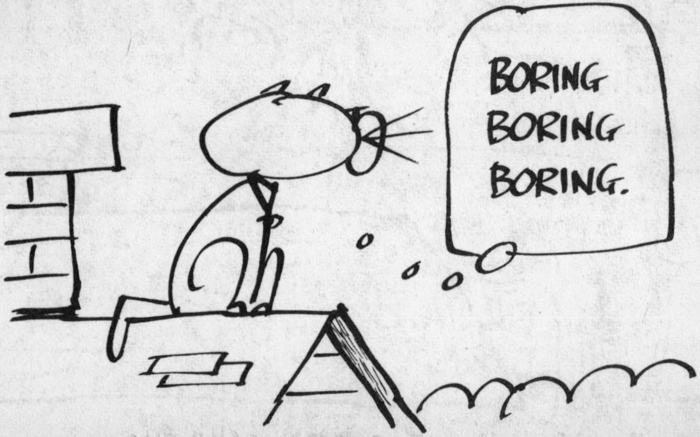
BORING BORING BORING.

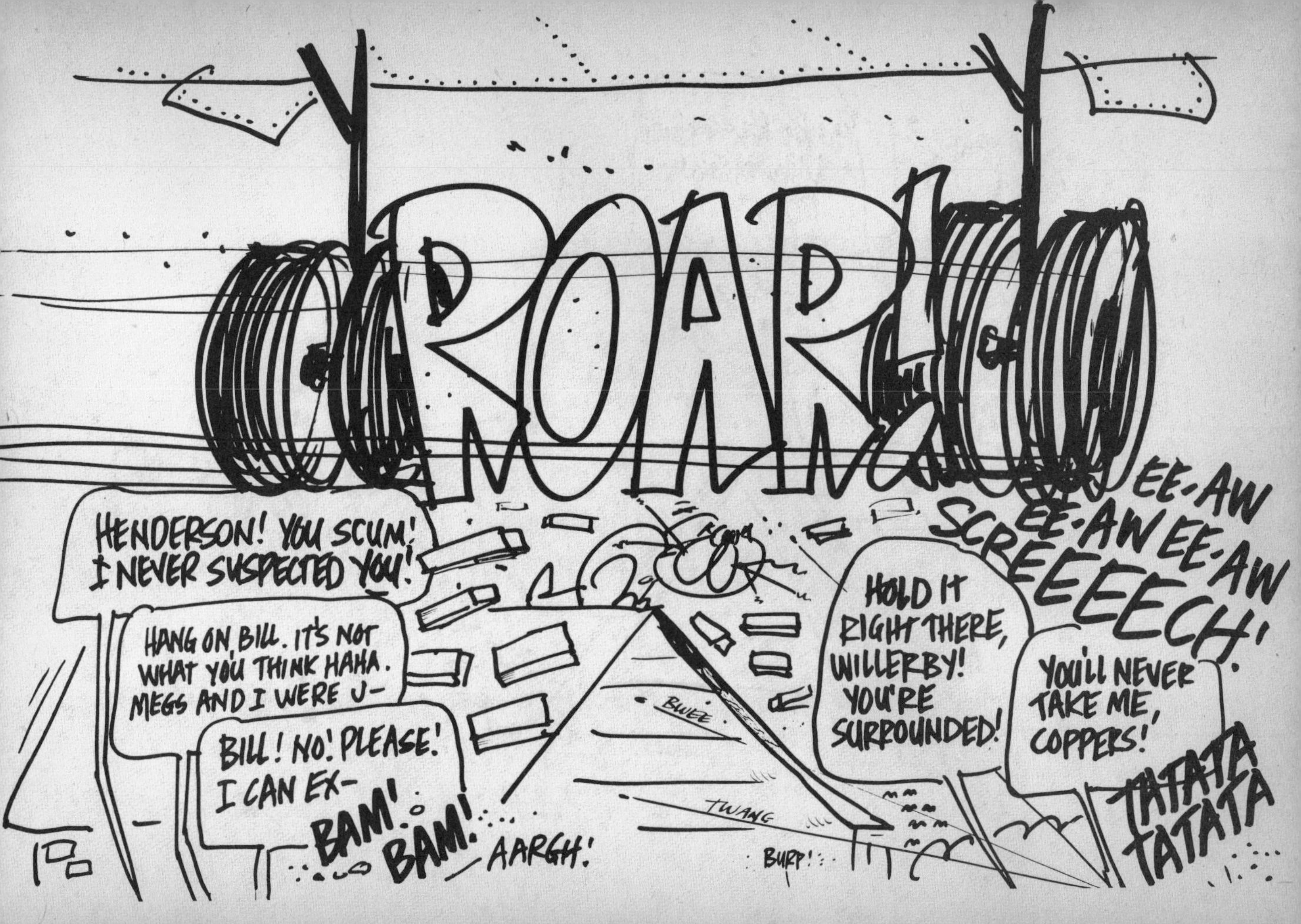
ROAR!
HENDERSON! YOU SCUM! I NEVER SUSPECTED YOU!
HANG ON BILL. IT'S NOT WHAT YOU THINK HAHA. MEGS AND I WERE J-
BILL! NO! PLEASE! I CAN EX-
BAM! BAM!
AARGH!
BWEE
TWANG
BURP!
EE-AW EE-AW EE-AW EE-AW
SCREEEEECH!
HOLD IT RIGHT THERE, WILLERBY! YOU'RE SURROUNDED!
YOU'LL NEVER TAKE ME, COPPERS!
TATATA TATATA

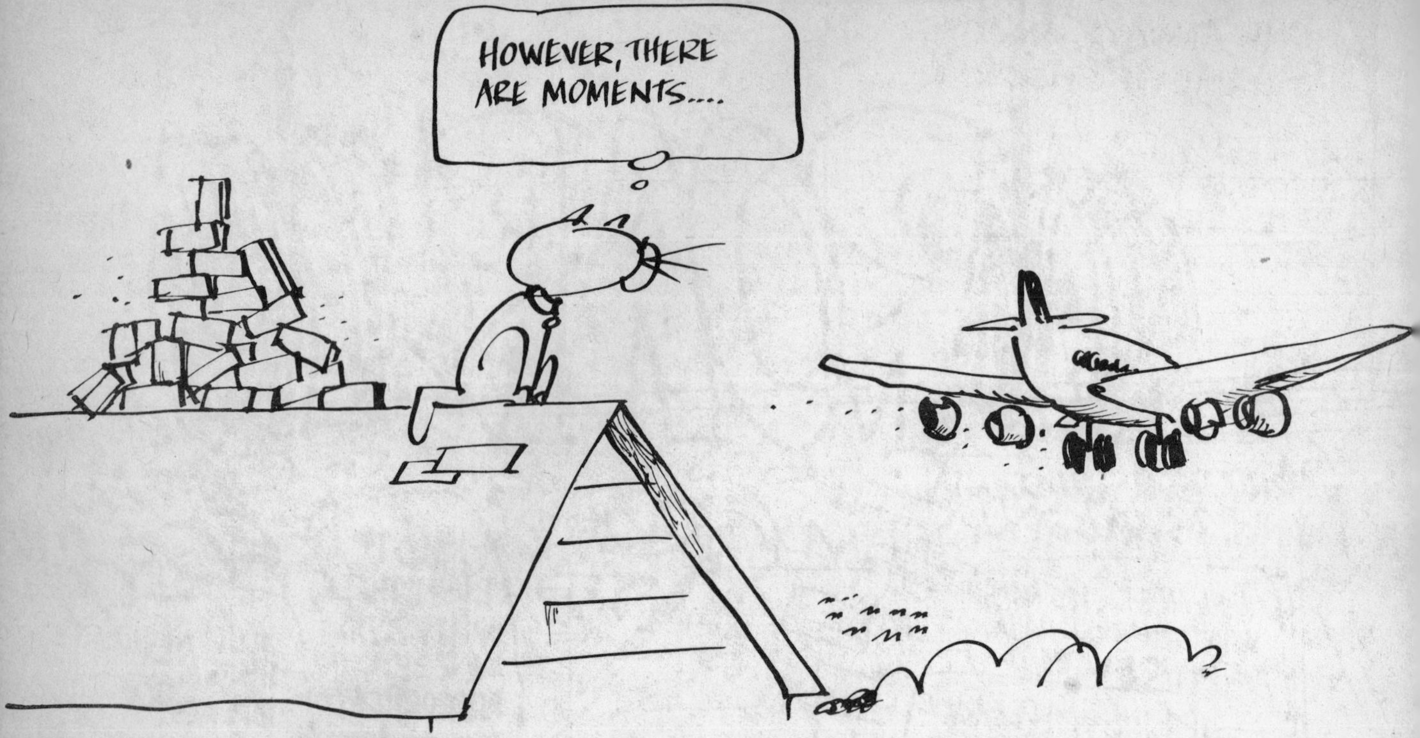
HOWEVER, THERE ARE MOMENTS....

Panel 1:
"ONE ALWAYS ENJOYS A GAME OF SNOOKER..."
"YOUR SHOT, PETE."

Panel 2:
"AND ALTHOUGH ONE CAN ONLY ASSUME THE ROLL OF SPECTATOR..."
CLIK!
"GO BABY!"

SOMETIMES ONE CAN FIND AN OPPORTUNITY...
GO! GO! GO!
CLAMP!
TO AFFECT THE OUTCOME OF SOMEONE ELSE'S GAME.
SNAP

HEY! SHE'S CUTE!
FERNLEA TENNIS CLUB
BOUNCE BOUNCE
VERY CUTE INDEED.

UGH!
BAM
WHAZZ
FUNNY HOW THEY CAN LOSE ALL THEIR SEX APPEAL IN ONE SERVE.
STOMP STOMP STOMP

THERE GOES POOR OL' MAX. THEY TOOK HIM TO THE VET AND BINGO HE WASN'T A 'TOM' ANYMORE...
HE USED TO BE A TEN-TO-FIFTEEN-TIMES-A-NIGHT CAT. NOW HE JUST GOES HOME AN' WATCHES TV.

(SIGH)... THAT'S THE TROUBLE WITH A VASECTOMY.... IT'S SO FINAL...
SO TERRIBLY, CRUELLY FINAL....

BEFORE WE GO OFF ON OUR HONEYMOON, MANDY, THERE'S SOME-THING YOU SHOULD KNOW!
WHAT IS IT, BOGART, MY DARLING?
I- I'M ONLY HALF A CAT.
YOU MEAN... THE WAR?...
NO... I MEAN THE VET.
THEN (SIGH) I'M AFRAID IT'S 'GOOD-BYE'....

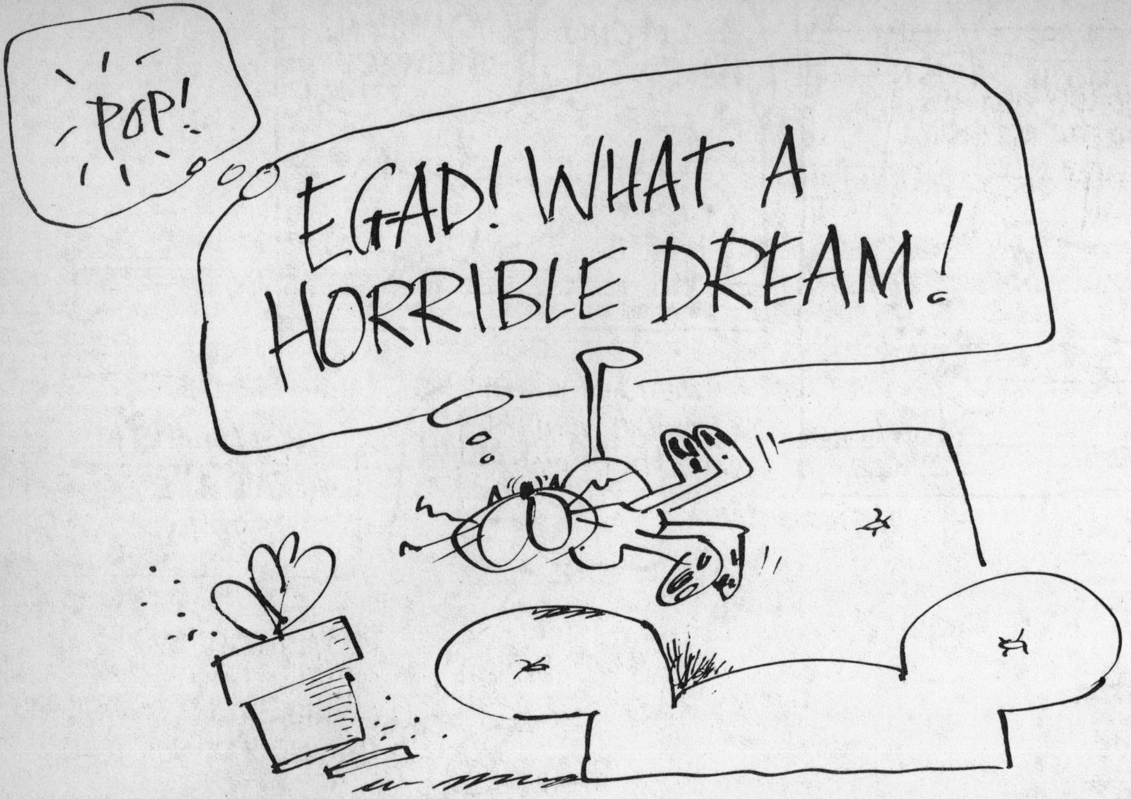
POP!
EGAD! WHAT A HORRIBLE DREAM!

THERE'S NO WAY THEY'D GET ME IN FOR THE SNIP.
NO WAY...
ASIDE FROM ALL THAT FUN WITH FELINES GOIN' OUT THE WINDOW, WHAT IF I WANTED TO START A FAMILY, HMM?
THE FACT THAT I'VE STARTED TWENTY-TWO FAMILIES IN THIS STREET ALONE IS NEITHER HERE NOR THERE.

DAMN! THERE MUST BE A WAY I CAN STOP BECOMIN' A FATHER EVERY TIME I WANNA HAVE A LITTLE FUN.
WAITAMINNIT! I'LL USE THE 'RHYTHM METHOD'!
WHAT A GREAT IDEA!!
WHY JUST THE OTHER DAY I HEARD SOME GUY SAYIN' HE USED THE RHYTHM METHOD! IF HE CAN USE IT, SO CAN I!

BOY OH BOY OH BOY! THE GOOD OL' RHYTHM METHOD! WHY DIDN'T I THINK OF THAT BEFORE?

A COUPLE WEEKS LATER:
WHAT? BUT HOW COULD YOU BE!!?? I USED THE RHYTHM METHOD!!

INCREDIBLE! ABSOLUTELY INCREDIBLE! WHAT COULD HAVE GONE WRONG?
MAYBE I WAS USIN' THE WRONG RHYTHM! BUT I DON'T SEE WHAT'S WRONG WITH USIN' A SLOW BOOGIE. WHAT'S WRONG WITH USIN' A SLOW BOOGIE??
TROUBLE IS, I COULDN'T BE SERIOUS IF I HAD TO DO IT TO A CHA-CHA. HAHAHA!

HAHAHAHA!
ONE-TWO-CHA-CHA-CHA!
ONE-TWO-CHA-CHA-CHA!
HAHAHAHARHOHO
HAHAHOOHOOHAHA
HOHOHOOHOOHOO!
ALL KIDDING ASIDE, I'LL TRY DOIN' IT TO `YOU SAY PO-TAY-TOE AN' I SAY PO-TAH-TOE' AND IF THAT DOESN'T WORK TO HELL WITH THE RHYTHM METHOD!

THERE'S A PEANUT LYIN' DOWN THERE, ED. I'M GONNA—
HOLD IT, CHARLIE. HERE COMES THAT CAT.
FLAP FLAP
FLAP
I'LL WAIT'LL HE GOES BY. NO SENSE IN— HEY! HE ATE IT! HE ATE THE GUDDAM PEANUT!!!
I DON'T GET IT. CAT'S DON'T LIKE PEANUTS!
I JUST LIKE TO ANNOY PEOPLE.

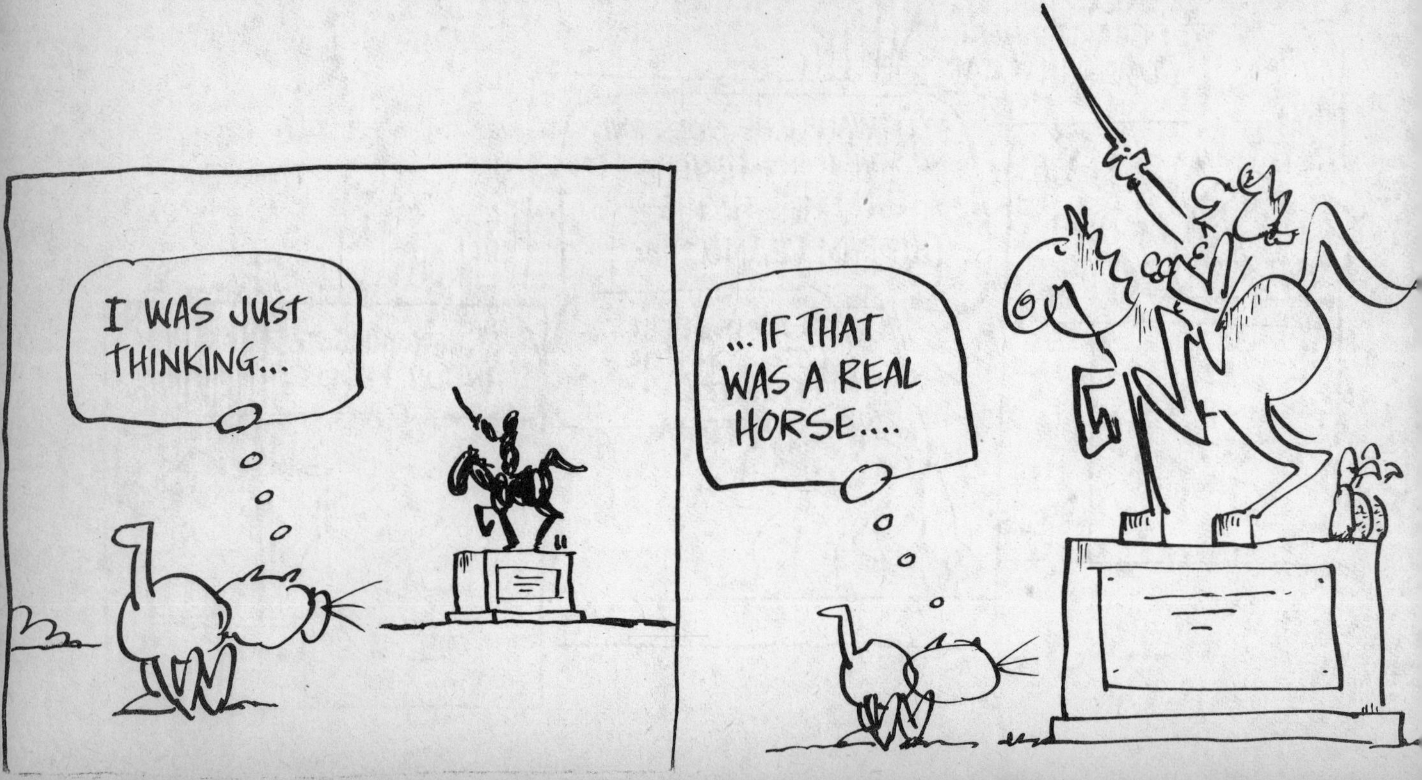
I WAS JUST THINKING...
...IF THAT WAS A REAL HORSE....

THAT WOULDN'T BE A TERRIFIC PLACE FOR THOSE TWO PIGEONS TO BE SITTING.

I'M DETERMINED NOT TO LET THAT CAT GET AWAY WITH STEALING MY PEANUT.
SO?
SO I'M GONNA FLY LOW THROUGH THE CITY UNTIL I SPOT HIM, AND THEN... KER-SPLATTO!
GOOD LUCK, CHARLIE.
FLAP
FLAP
FLAP
TEN MINUTES LATER:
CHARLIE! WHAT HAPPENED?!
THEY... THEY'VE ..(WHEEZE).. PUT DOUBLE DECKER BUSES... ON F-F-FERNLEA STREET....
ARGH!

I'VE GOT IT, ED! I PUT A PEANUT UNDER A TREE. I HIDE IN THE TREE AND WHEN THE CAT COMES TO TAKE THE PEANUT, SPLAT!, I GETTIM!
GO FOR IT, CHARLIE!
SEE YOU LATER, ED.
FLAP FLAP FLAP
TEN MINUTES LATER:
FLAP FLAP FLAP FLAP
CHARLIE! WHAT HAPPENED??
IT'S A LONG STORY, ED, BUT BASICALLY YOU SHOULD NEVER PICK A TREE WITH THREE OR MORE CROWS IN IT.

WOW! THIS IS SKATEBOARDIN' WEATHER!
HERE I GO!.... OOPS! I'LL CIRCUMNAVIGATE THAT OBSTACLE APPROACHING FROM THE LEFT.
ZAP
TAXI!
ZAZ
KRACK!
BWEEEEEE
DURING THE WINTER LAY-OFF YOUR SENSE OF TIMING GETS A LITTLE RUSTY.
ZAP

HEY! HERE'S A HILL I'VE NEVER TRIED.
MEANWHILE
...AND THEN THERE WAS THE MORNING OF JULY 8, 1944... WE WERE SOMEWHERE OVER THE CHANNEL.... BILL HAD A PIECE OF SHRAPNEL IN HIS LEG... SUDDEN-
CRASH!
YARGH!
TWAZZZ
THAT'S RIGHT!! MESSERSCHMITTS! FORTY OR FIFTY OF THEM!!!

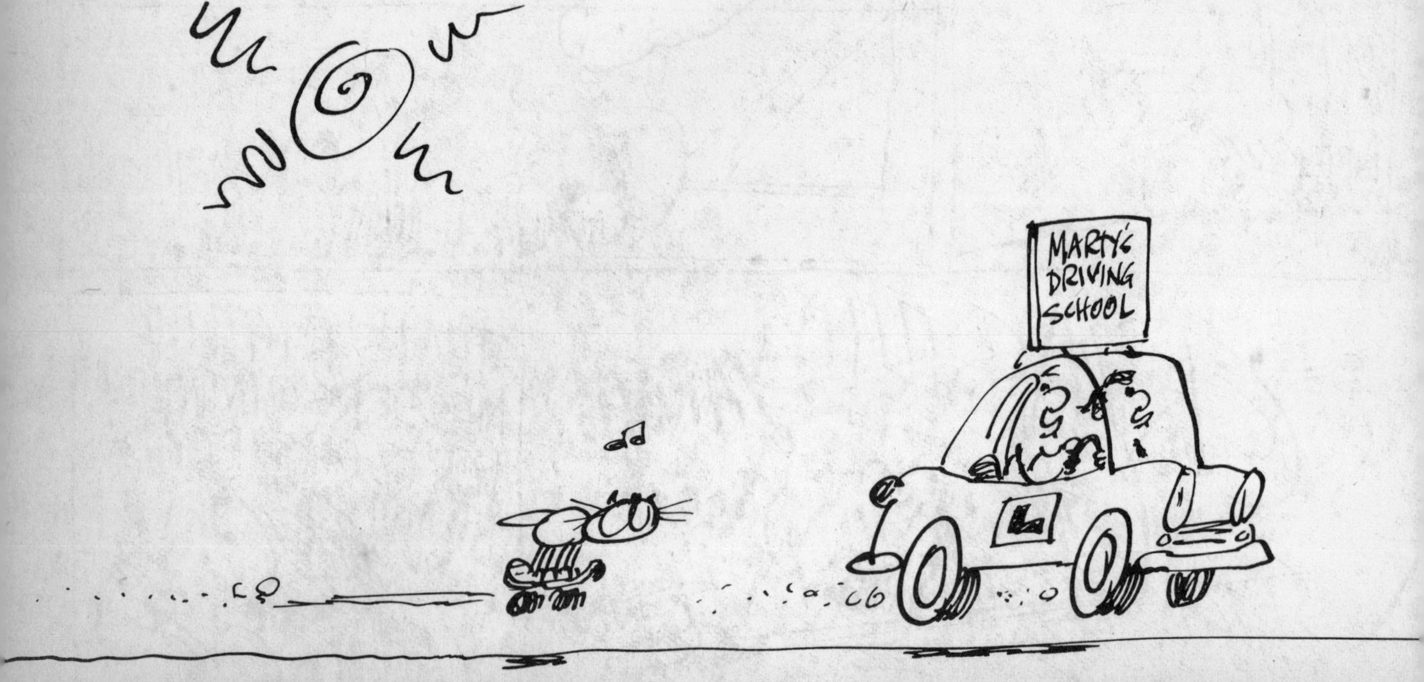
MARTY'S
DRIVING
SCHOOL
L

WHAT DO I DO IF I SEE I'M BEING FOLLOWED BY A CAT ON A SKATEBOARD?

GUN IT AND RACE HIM BACK TO THE DRIVING SCHOOL.

ARGH!

GUNNNNNNN

GAROARRR

FLANG

ANOTHER MILD
ONE, ISN'T IT.

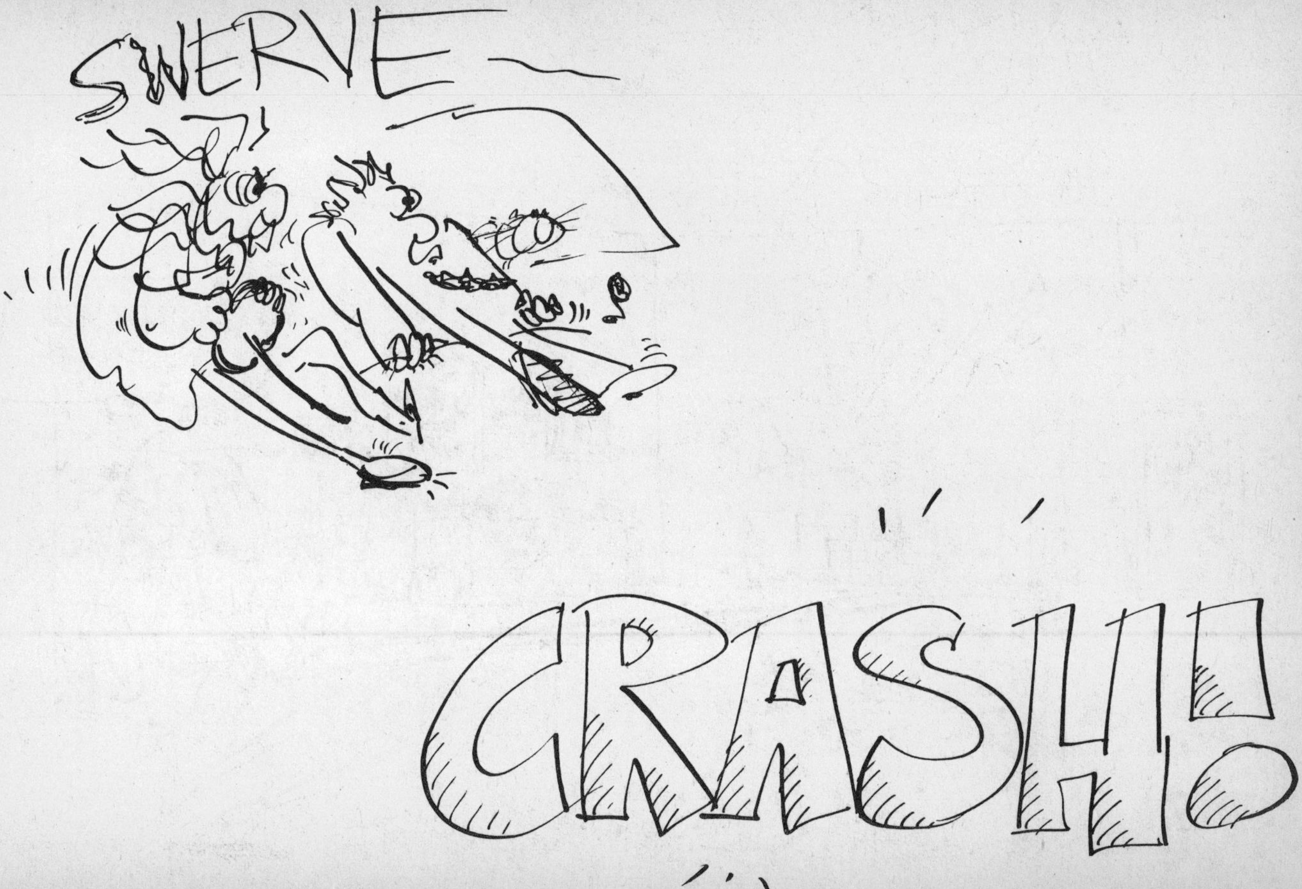
SWERVE
CRASH!

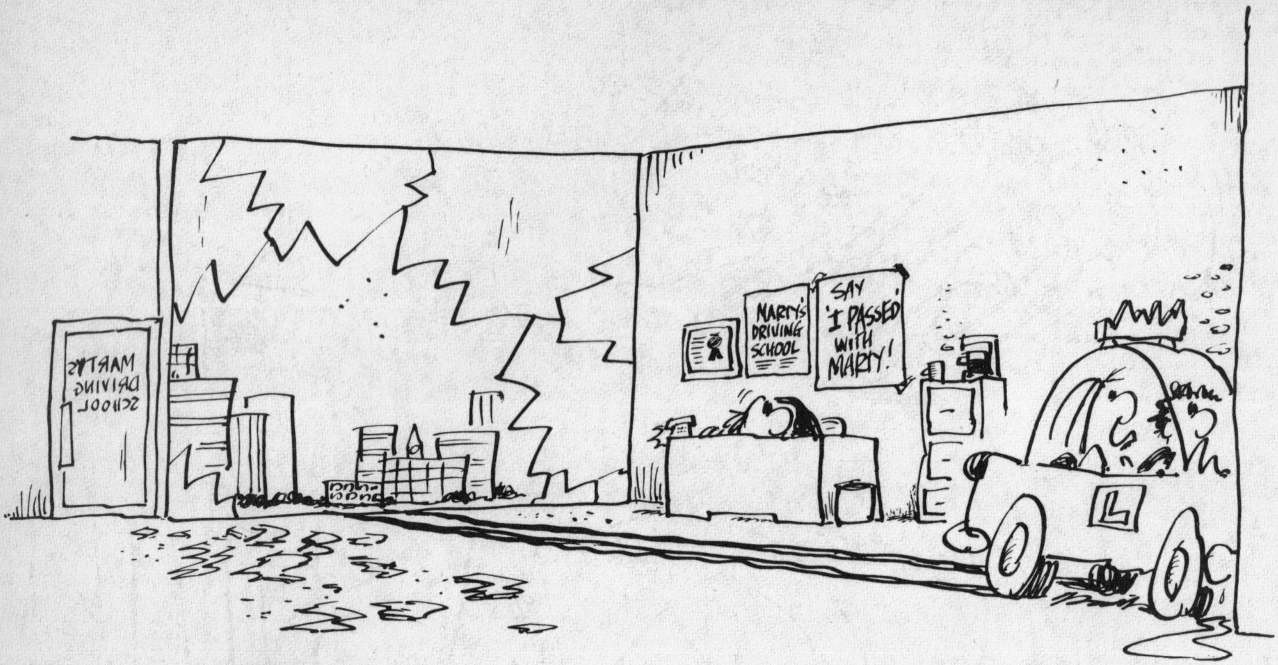
MARTY'S DRIVING SCHOOL
SAY 'I PASSED' WITH MARTY!
L

.... I'M NOT SAYIN' I DON'T BELIEVE THE (COUGH!) STORY ABOUT THE CAT ON THE SKATEBOARD, ANDY, I'M JUST SAYIN' IT MIGHT BE A GOOD IDEA IF YOU TOOK A LITTLE TIME OFF.... RENT A CAR.... GO FOR A DRIVE UP THE COAST.... RELAX....

MUMBLE.... MUMBLE...
'CAT ONNA GODDAM SKATEBOARD'...
MUMBLE... MUMBLE.... OUT
OF HIS GODDAM TREE....
MARTY'S DRIVING SCHOOL
SLAM
RRRRRRRRRRR-
VAROOM
VAROOM
MUMBLE
MUMBLE
GRIND!
ROARRRR

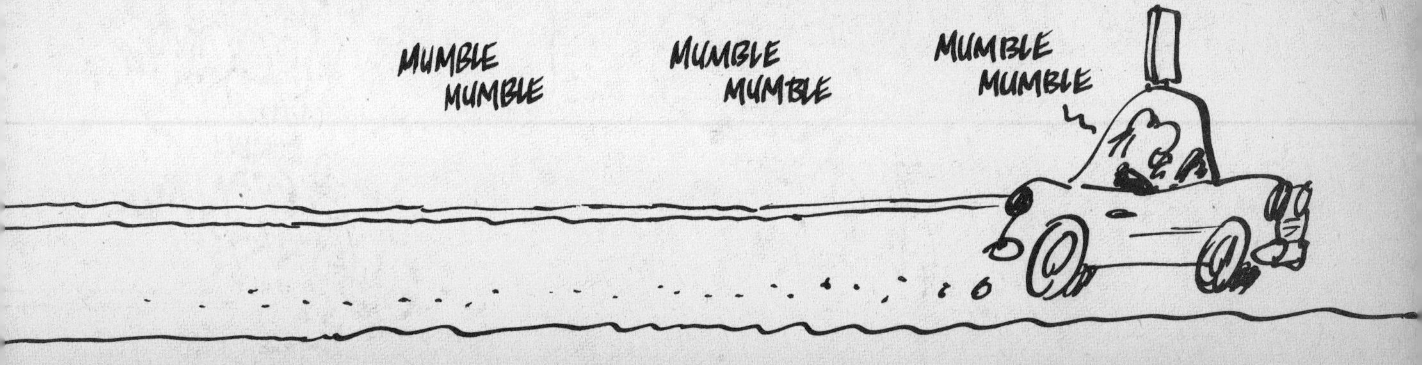
MUMBLE MUMBLE
MUMBLE MUMBLE
MUMBLE MUMBLE

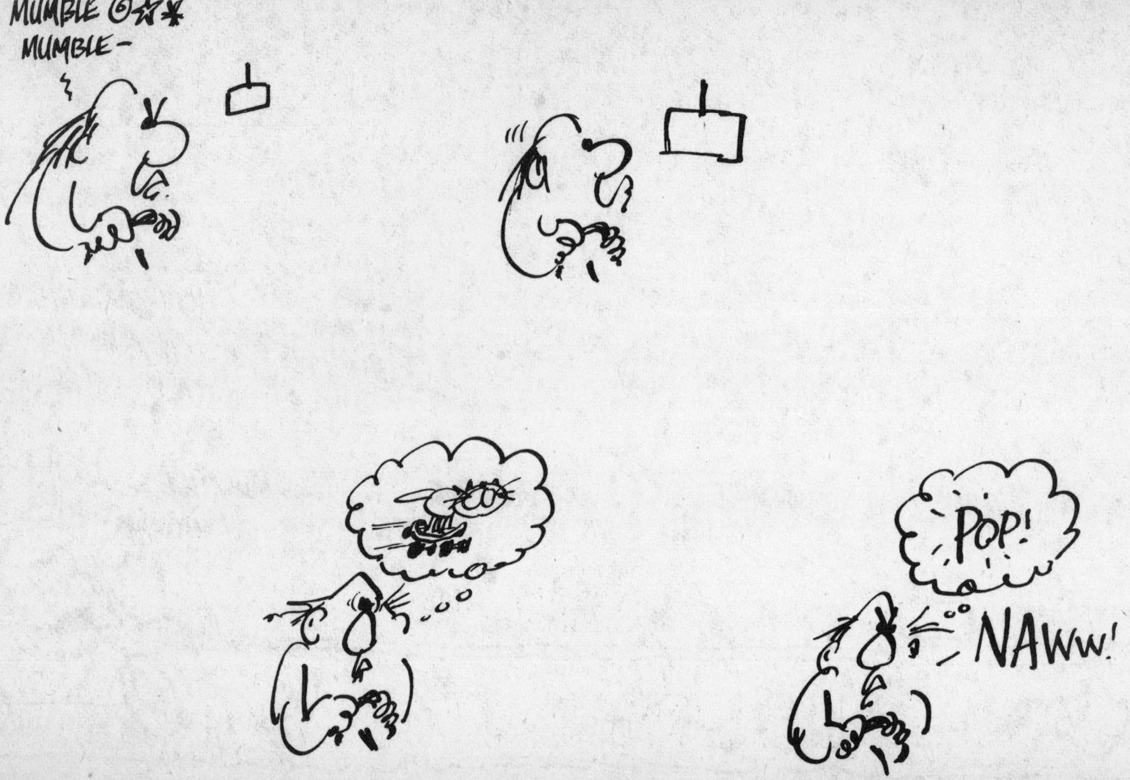
MUMBLE ◎☆✱
MUMBLE-
POP!
NAWW!

AARGH!!!
IT IS!!!
NO GODDAM CAT IS GONNA MAKE AN IDIOT OUTA ME!!
GUNNNNN
FLAM

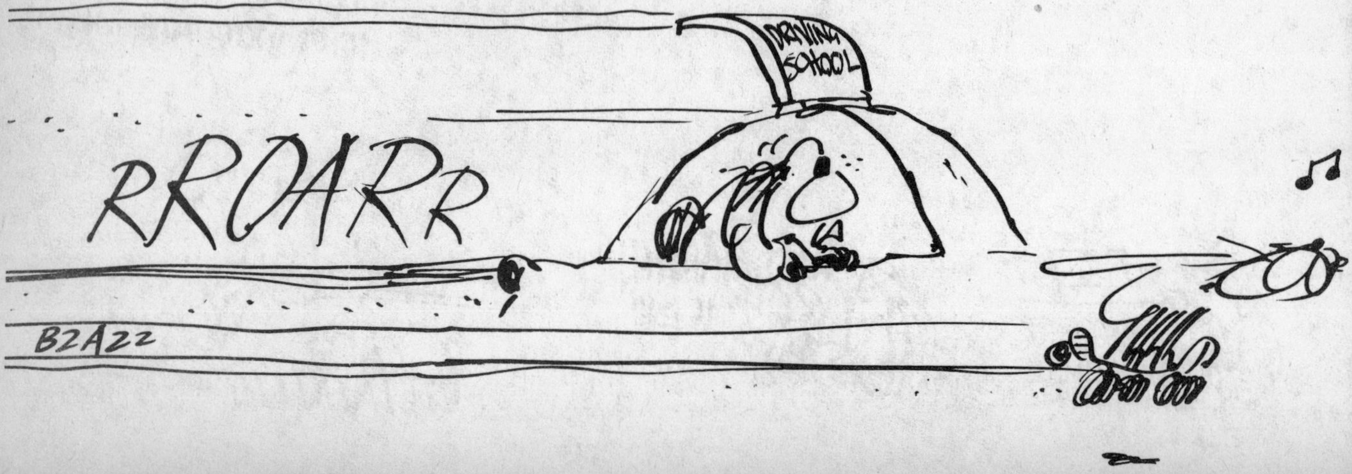
DRIVING SCHOOL
RROARR
BZAZZ

I DON'T SUPPOSE YOU'D GO FOR THE STORY THAT I WAS BEING FOLLOWED BY A CAT ON A SKATEBOARD.
POLICE

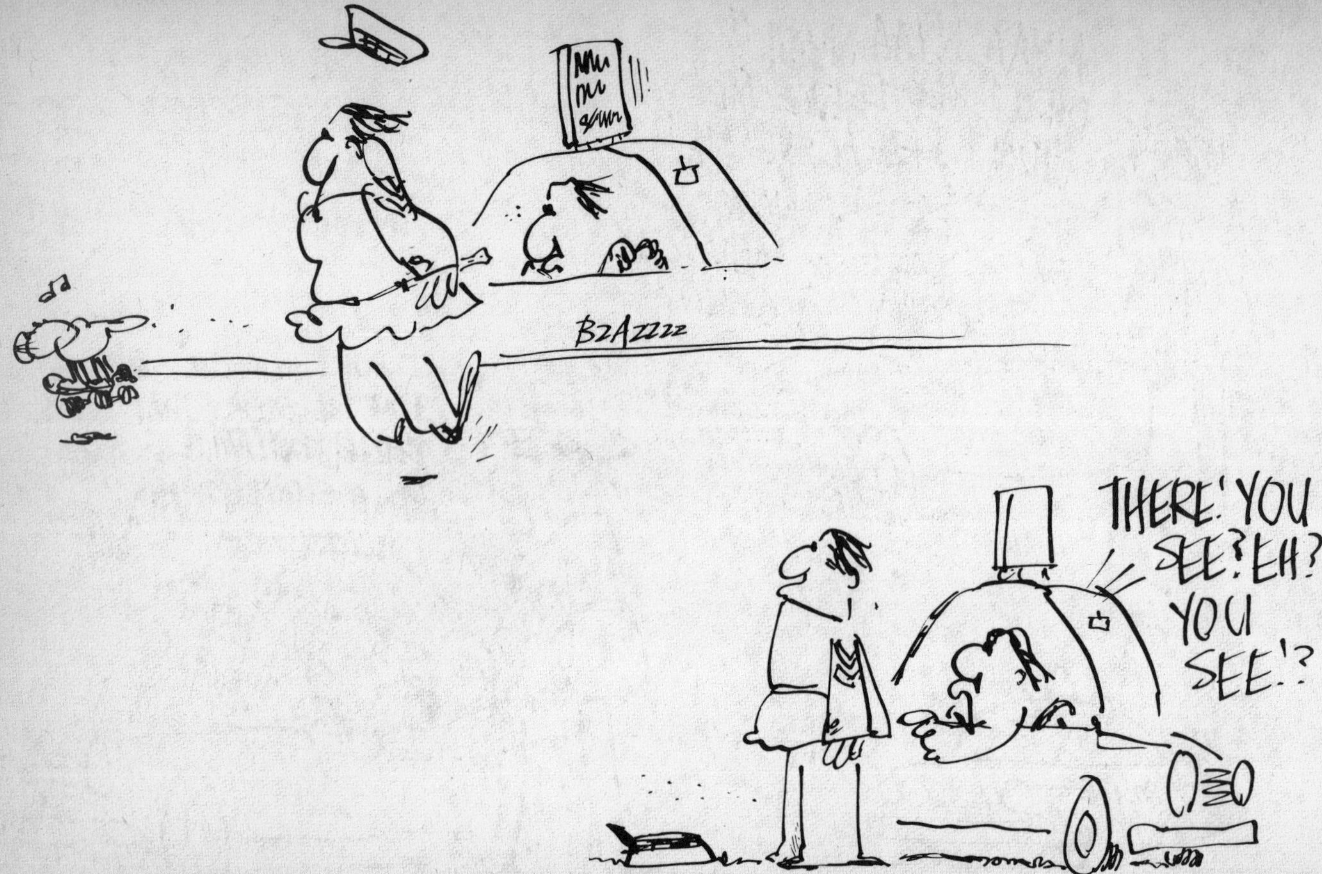
BZAZZZZ
THERE! YOU SEE? EH? YOU SEE!?

NYAA NYAA NYAA!!
DIDN'T BEE-LEEVE ME!
DIDN'T BEE-LEEVE ME!
NOW WHATCHA GONNA DOO-HOO?!
RIGHT! YOU'RE NICKED FOR NOT HAVIN' A SEAT BELT ON!!!

OH, YEAH? WELL THIS IS A CARTOON STRIP AND THE SEAT BELT LAW DOESN'T APPLY TO PEOPLE IN CARTOON STRIPS! NYA! SO THERE!

LOOK! IN A CARTOON STRIP I CAN STICK MY BUM OUT AT A COP! HAHA! IN A CARTOON STRIP YOU CAN DO ANY-

WHUMP!

WHAT HAPPENED BACK THERE, BOB?

I ALWAYS WANTED TO KICK ONE OF THOSE GUYS IN THE ASS.

ED. DO ME A FAVOUR. LOOK TO THE LEFT AN' TELL ME IF YOU SEE ANYTHING COMIN'.
NOPE. NOTHIN'.
OKAY. NOW LOOK TO THE RIGHT.
NOOP. NOT A THING.
OKAY. I'M GONNA NIP DOWN AN' GRAB THAT PEANUT.
UH... HOLD IT, CHARLIE. I THINK I SEE...
NIP
KAZ-FLANG!
... A CAT ON A SKATEBOARD.
OHHHNNG...

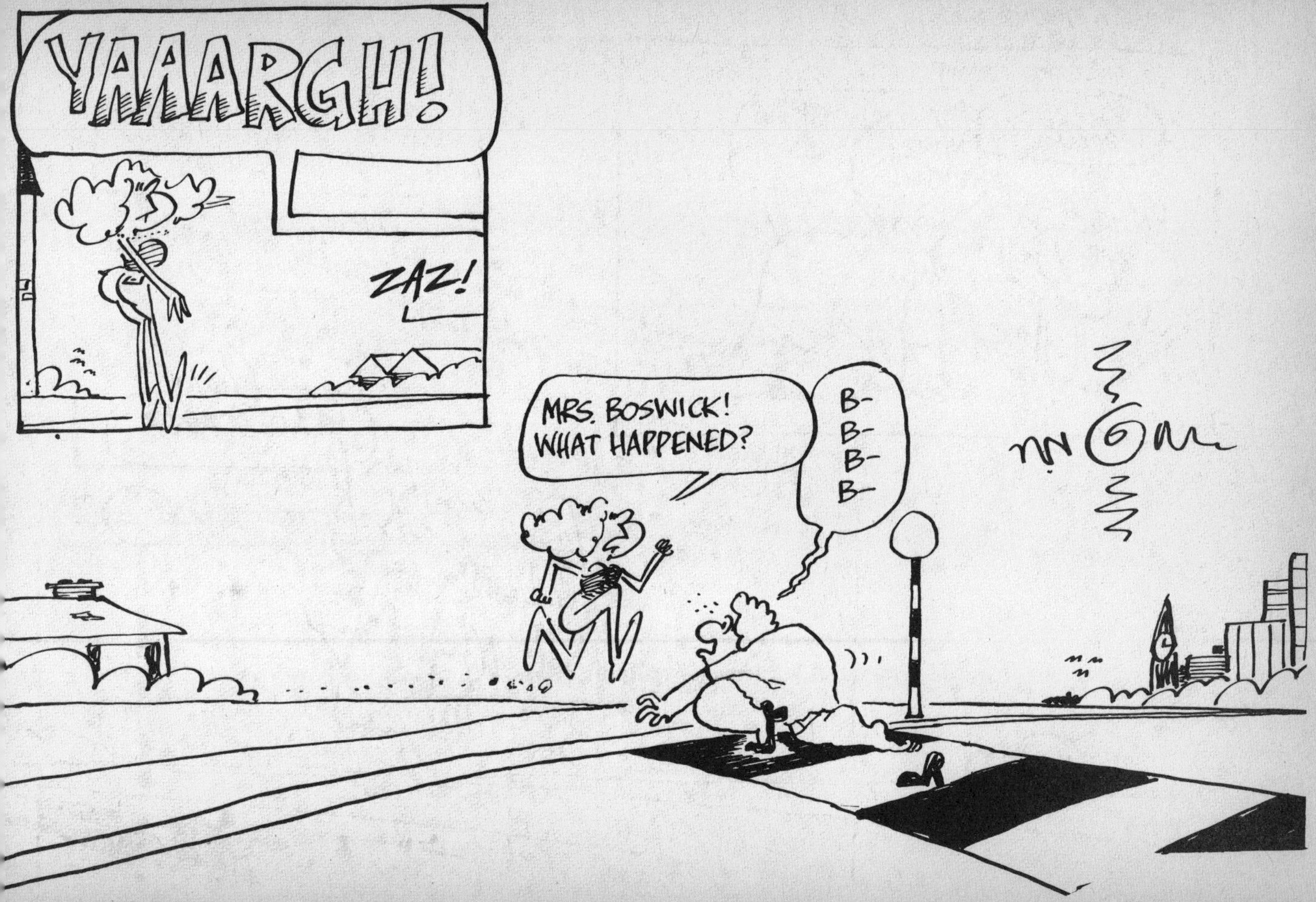
YAAARGH!
ZAZ!
MRS. BOSWICK! WHAT HAPPENED?
B- B- B- B-

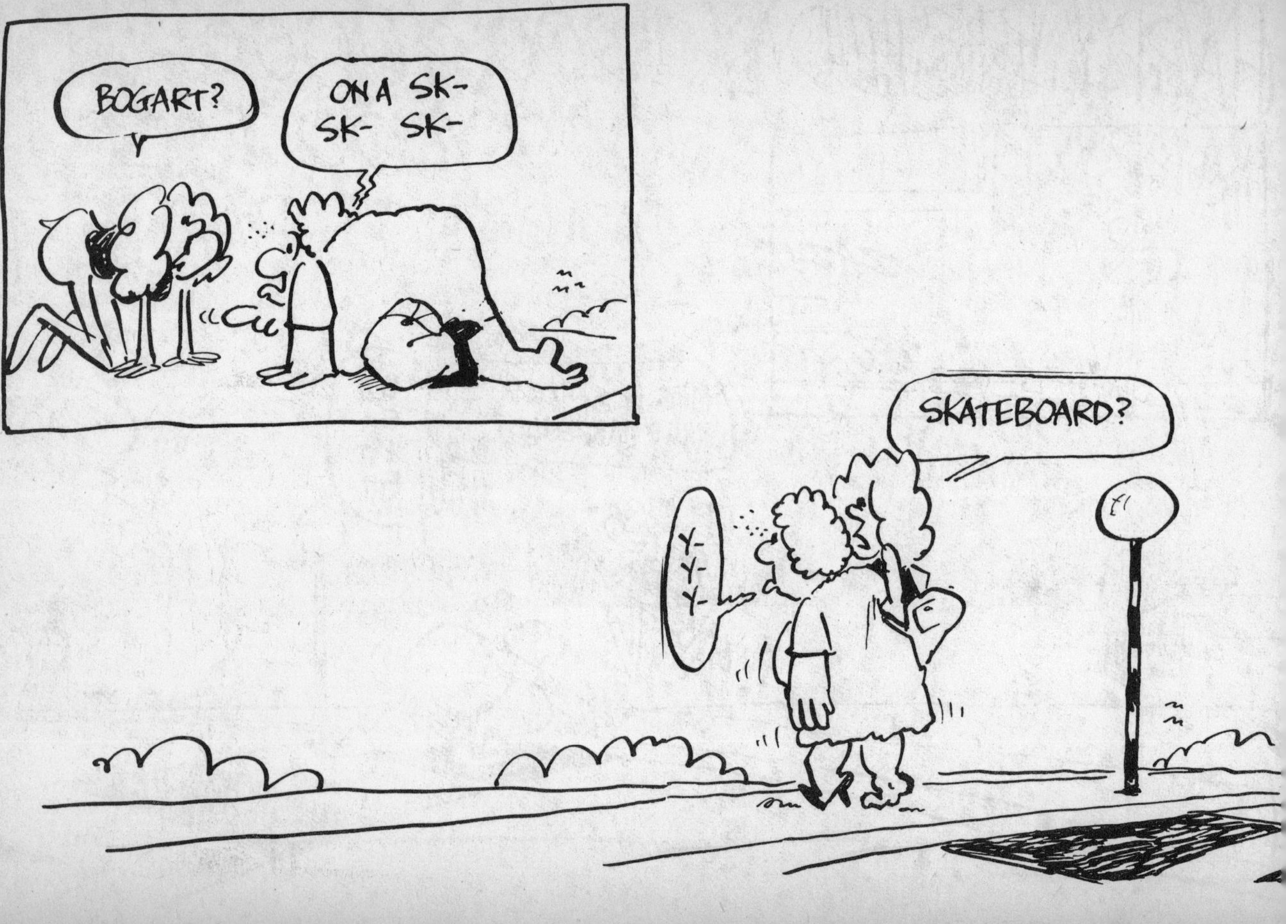
BOGART?
ON A SK- SK- SK-
Y- Y- Y-
SKATEBOARD?

HAPPY BIRTHDAY TOOO YOOOO ♪♫♪
HAPPY BIRTHDAY TOOO YOOO ♪♫♪
HAPPY BIRTHDAY DEAR UNCLE BARNEEEE

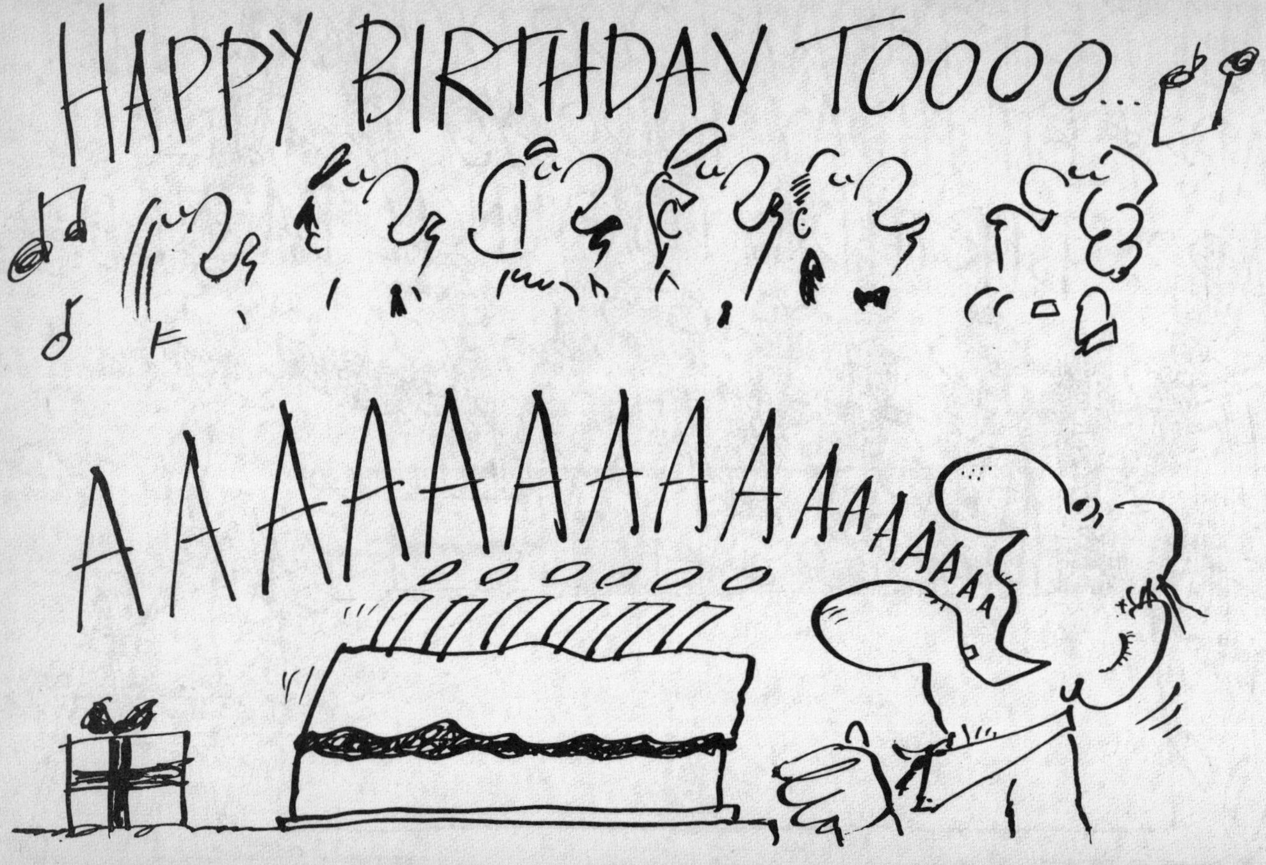
HAPPY BIRTHDAY TOOOOO...
AAAAAAAAAAAAAAAAAAA

WHAZ!

TELL YOU ONE THING. THE OLD GEEZER CAN STILL BLOW!

ER... I'M SORRY, MISS. BUT WE'VE GOT ORDERS TO CONFISCATE YOUR CAT'S SKATEBOARD.
YOU DOITY RATS.
HE'S BEEN TERRORIZING THE NEIGHBOURHOOD ON IT. THERE'VE BEEN A NUMBER OF COMPLAINTS.
YOU DOITY DOITY RATS.
IT'S OUT BACK. BESIDE THE DUST-BINS...
FLIP!
AAAAAAAA
CRASH!
ARGH!
TINKLE!
BESIDE MY MARBLE COLLECTION.
OFFICER?

ERRRRR
RRRRRRRRR
RRRRK!
SOME DAY YOU'RE GONNA MISJUDGE YOUR STOPPING DISTANCE AN' HIT THE PUB!
LAMB AN' FLAG

TELL YOU WHAT, BOG', OL' FELLA. THERE'S A MOUSE SOMEWHERE IN THIS PUB. IF YOU CAN CATCH HIM I'LL BUY YOU A BEER!
TWANGGGGGGGG
WHALLOP!
OKAY. THAT TAKES CARE OF THE MOUSE. NOW WHERE'S MY BEER?

LISTEN, BOG. YOU'VE HAD A FEW. DO YA THINK IT'S A GOOD IDEA TO GET ONTO THAT SKATEBOARD?
HE'S RIGHT YOU KNOW. I'M PRETTY ZONKED.
OL' GROVER HERE'LL TAKE YOU HOME, WON'T YOU FELLA.
LAMB AN' FLAG
IT'S NICE TO KNOW A PUB WITH A CAB SERVICE.

CHUCK'S COSTUME SHOP
DELIVERIES ONLY →
HEY! SOMEONE TOSSED OUT A CAPE AN' A MASK!
I LIKE IT, CHUCK. I LIKE IT A LOT.

I'LL STALK THE CITY STREETS AT NIGHT STRIKING FEAR AN' TERROR INTO PEOPLE EVERYWHERE!! NO ONE WILL BE SAFE FROM
THE PHANTOM!

THE CITY STREETS ARE DARK AND EMPTY.... EMPTY, THAT IS, EXCEPT FOR 'THE PHAN—
YAARGH!!
A REFLECTION IN A SHOP WINDOW (AHEM) MOMENTARILY DISTRACTS 'THE PHANTOM'.

CONCEALED IN HIS TREE HIDE-OUT, 'THE PHANTOM' WAITS FOR HIS NEXT VICTIM...
AHA!
♫
ONE... TWO... THREE...
AARGH!
I'VE GOT TO WORK MORE ON MY 'TERRORIZING LEAP.'

(CHUCKLE) CLEVERLY CONCEALED BY THE FOLIAGE OF HIS TREE-LAIR, 'THE PHANTOM' IS READY TO STRIKE...
BOGART, YOU COME DOWN FROM THAT TREE THIS MINUTE YOU SILLY CAT!!
HMM. MAYBE THE TREE-LAIR COULD DO WITH A BIT MORE FOLIAGE.

LOOKING FOR A NEW HIDE-OUT, 'THE PHANTOM' FINDS A CLUMP OF BUSHES.
MEOYKS!
REOWR!
I KEEP FORGETTING TONY AND LOUISE USE THOSE BUSHES.

AS 'THE PHANTOM' WAITS FOR HIS NEXT VICTIM, HE CAN'T HELP NOTICING THE AUTUMN NIGHTS ARE GETTING CHILLY...
SHIVER
SHIVER
SHIVER
SHIVER
SHIVER
SHIVER
SHIVER
HE ALSO CAN'T HELP NOTICING HE'S BLOWN HIS COVER.

LET'S GO HOME, KEVIN. WHAT IF 'THE PHANTOM'-
CHUCKLE. I'LL TAKE CARE OF THE-
EEEEEEEEEE
AAAAAAAAA!
YOU BIG CHICKEN! IT WAS A CAT!!!
N-N-N- B-B-B- WA-WA-WOO- G-G-G-
ROARRR

Y'KNOW WHAT I THINK, BOB? I THINK THIS 'PHANTOM' THING IS A LOAD OF—
ANDY...
POLICE
... ANDY, I'M LOOKING IN THE REAR-VIEW MIRROR AND I'M SEEING HIM, ANDY, I'M SEEING THE 'PHANTOM'....
OKAY, BOB. YOU HIT HIM HIGH AND I'LL HIT HIM LOW... ONE... TWO....
....THREE!
WHAM!
ARRGH!
GOTCHA YA LITTLE—
SORRY, ANDY... IT- IT MUSTA BEEN THE HAT... I THOUGHT...
OOOOO OOOOO OOOH!
JOGGING CLUB

JUST A CAUTIONARY WARNING, MISS, TO BE ON THE LOOKOUT FOR A MASKED CAT WHO'S BEEN TERRORISING THE NEIGHBOURHOOD. HE CALLS HIMSELF 'THE PHANTOM'.
AAAEEEE
THAT WAS A DIFFICULT PERFORMANCE, BUT IT PROBABLY ELIMINATED ME FROM THE LIST OF SUSPECTS.

I GOT HIM, BARNEY! I GOT 'THE PHANTOM'!
LET'S TAKE OFF HIS MASK AN' SEE WHO HE IS!
DEY NICKED ME FAIR AN' SQUARE.
WANTED
TOUR OF WORMWOOD SCRUBS!
WELL I'LL BE-
IT'S A CAT!
YOU WERE EXPECTING MAYBE JULIO IGLESIAS?
MINICAB
SHIRLEY
TERESA
POLICE 999
HELLO, THIS IS FERNLEA POLICE STATION...
...AND ANYTHING YOU SAY MAY BE TAKEN DOWN AND...
I WANNA SEE MY LAWYER.

'DOSE DOITY RATZ COULDN'TA HELD ME FOR LONG. I WUZ ALREADY STARTIN' ON A TUNNEL.
POLICE

"ALL READY FOR THE BIG FROG RACE TOMORROW IN FERNLEA PARK, QUINCE'?"

"RIBBIT"

"GONNA BEAT THE PACK? HM? GONNA PULL ON THOSE OL' WEBBERS LIKE YOU NEVER PULLED BEFORE? HM?"

"RIBBIT"

GONNA GO-GO-GO FOR GOLD? HUH, BIG FELLA?
RIBBIT
HE SEEMS TO BE PRETTY PSYCHED UP FOR THE EVENT, IN ANY CASE.
RIBBIT

FERNLEA PARK
ANNUAL
FROG RACE
RIBBIT RIBBIT RIBBIT RIBBIT RIBBIT RIBBIT RIBBIT ROBBIT RIBBIT RIBBIT RIBBIT RIBBIT RIBBIT RIBBIT RIBBIT RIBBIT
BLAH BLAH BLAH BLAH BLAH BLAH BLAH BLAH BLAH BLAH BLAH BLAH BLAH
RIBBIT
WOW! I'VE NEVER SEEN SO MANY FROGS!

RIBBIT RIBBIT
RIBBIT

OY! QUINCY! YOU'RE HERE TO WIN A RACE, NOT SOCIALIZE!!
RIBBIT RIBBIT RIBBIT RIBBIT
RABBIT ROBBIT RUBBIT GRABBIT

Panel 1: THE FERNLEA PARK FROG RACE IS ABOUT TO START. BOGART IS GIVING QUINCY SOME LAST-MINUTE INSTRUCTIONS.

"MEOWR FROWR MWOWR..."

"RIBBIT."

Panel 2: "REOWR FWOWR BROWRR!"

"RIBBIT."

Panel 3: FERNLEA PARK ANIMAL FROG RACE

Panel 4: "I WAS TELLING QUINCY TO HANG BACK WITH THE REST OF THE PACK UNTIL THE LAST TEN METERS AND THEN MAKE HIS MOVE..."

RIBBIT

Panel 5: "TROUBLE IS, I DON'T KNOW WHAT 'RIBBIT' MEANS."

"ON YER MARK..."

"RIBBIT."

THEY'RE OFF!
BANG!
TWANGG
TWANG
TWANG
GO, QUINCY! SWIM YOU LITTLE SONOFABMMM
SPLASH!
SWIM
SWIM
SWIM
SWIM
SWIM
PARK
RACE
GO!
PULL!
ATTABOY!
SWIM!
GO!
GO!
GO!
GO!
YEAH!
OOPZ.
IN THE HEAT OF THE EVENT, A COACH CAN BE EXCUSED A LITTLE FOUL LANGUAGE.

HERE THEY COME AND IT'S QUINCY, THE WINNER!!
ATTABOY, QUINCE!
BONK
...NUMBER SEVEN, 'SLIMEY', IS SECOND.... 'CROAKER' IS THIRD... AND NUMBER TWELVE, THE FAVOURITE, 'CHARTREUSE BABY' IS FOURTH.
UH-OH. I WAS AFRAID OF THIS...
FERMLEA PARK ANNUAL FROG RACE
BURP
VICTORY HAS GONE TO HIS HEAD.
KICK
KICK
KICK

I DON'T CARE IF HE IS A CHAMPION RACING FROG, BOGART, YOU'RE NOT KEEPING HIM IN THE BATHTUB!
SPLISH
SPLASH
SPLASH
SPLASH
LATER THAT DAY:
RIBBIT.
ROZ?
GAGAGA
YOU OKAY, QUINCY?
RIBBIT.

I WONDER WHAT BOGART HAS DONE WITH THAT FROG.
RIBBIT.
EEEEEEEEEEEE!
TWANGGGGGGG
RIBBIT
OKAY! OKAY! BUT FROGS NEED SLEEP TOO, Y'KNOW.
RIBBIT.

SLAM!
WELL, HERE WE ARE, QUINCE', OUT IN THE COLD...
QUINCE'?
YE GODZ! HE'S FROZEN!
TINK TINK
FLIP
DON'T WORRY, BIG FELLA, WE'LL HAVE YOU THAWED OUT IN NO TIME!
WASH 'N DRY LAUNDRETTE
TINK
TINK
TINK
TINK
TINK

WASH 'N DRY LAUNDRETTE
DRYER
RIBBIT.
GOOD THING WE GOT HIM THAWED OUT OR ELSE OL' QUINCY, HERE, MIGHT'VE ENDED UP AS AN ORNAMENT ON SOME MANTELPIECE!! HAHAHAHAHA HAHAHAHA!!
FROGS AREN'T KNOWN FOR THEIR SENSE OF HUMOUR.

YOU WON'T STAY OFF THE BONNET OF MR. McILROY'S CAR SO I'M GOING TO LOCK YOU INDOORS!
MMP!

ROZ! I THINK HE'S GONNA BE SICK!!!

MMP!

IT'S AN OLD TRICK, BUT IT ALWAYS WORKS.

SLAM!

I WONDER HOW SHE'S SO SURE I'M THE FATHER. I'LL ASK HER......
MYOWR RROWR MEOWR?
YOWR?? RROWRR! FST! FWOWRR MEOWR! REOWR!
WHOOPS.
YEOWRR?? FSST! FSST!
MEOWR! FWROWR! REOWR!
MYOWR! MYOWR. FST! FST!
IT LOOKS PRETTY DEFINITE, ALL RIGHT.
HMF.

BOGART, I WANT A WORD WITH YOU.
UH-OH.
I KNOW YOU LIKE FOOLING AROUND WITH LOTS OF GIRLS, BUT WHEN YOU **DO**, YOU'VE GOT TO ACCEPT THE **RESPONSIBILITIES**!
THINK OF ALL THOSE POOR LITTLE KITTENS WAITING FOR THEIR DADDY TO TAKE THEM SOMEWHERE ON A SATURDAY AFTER-NOON!

THE GIRLS PROB'LY WOULD'VE PREFERRED A BALLET, BUT IT CAN'T BE HELPED.
FOOTBALL TODAY 3:00
FERNLEA MARAUDERS VS. GROTVILLE PANZERS
GATE 3
POLICE NOTICE
ABSOLUTELY NO UNNECESSARY VIOLENCE

KNOW SOMETHIN', ED? I GOT THE FEELIN' WE'RE BEIN' WATCHED.
YOU DO?
YEAH. I DUNNO WHY, BUT I JUST GOT THAT FEELIN', KNOW WHAT I MEAN?
WELL, THERE'S NOBODY AROUND EXCEPT YOU, ME, AND THE STATUE UP THERE, CHARLIE. HAHAHAHA!
YEAH. I GUESS IT'S JUST ME BEIN' PARANOID AGAIN, HAHAHAHA!
YEAH. HAHAHA.

HI. I'M STEVEN SPEELBURP, THE BIG FILM DIRECTOR. I WAS WONDERING IF YOU COULD HELP US OUT OVER AT THE STUDIO.
YOU NEED A SEXY NEW FEMALE LEAD!
ER...NO. WE NEED A CAT.
A CAT?

BEFORE I SAY 'YES', LET ME HAVE A LOOK AT THE SCRIPT
AHH!

THE FILM IS CALLED "THE SEVEN SINS OF CYNTHIA". YOU PLAY "BINKY", CYNTHIA'S CAT.
ROLL 'EM.

OKAY... CYNTHIA... HYSTERICAL WITH GRIEF FOR NICO.... AAAND.... ACTION!
WHIRRRRRR
OH, NEE-CO, SOB..
IT'S NOT A BIG PART BUT AT LEAST I GET TO SPEND SOME TIME ON A BED WITH BO DINKLE.

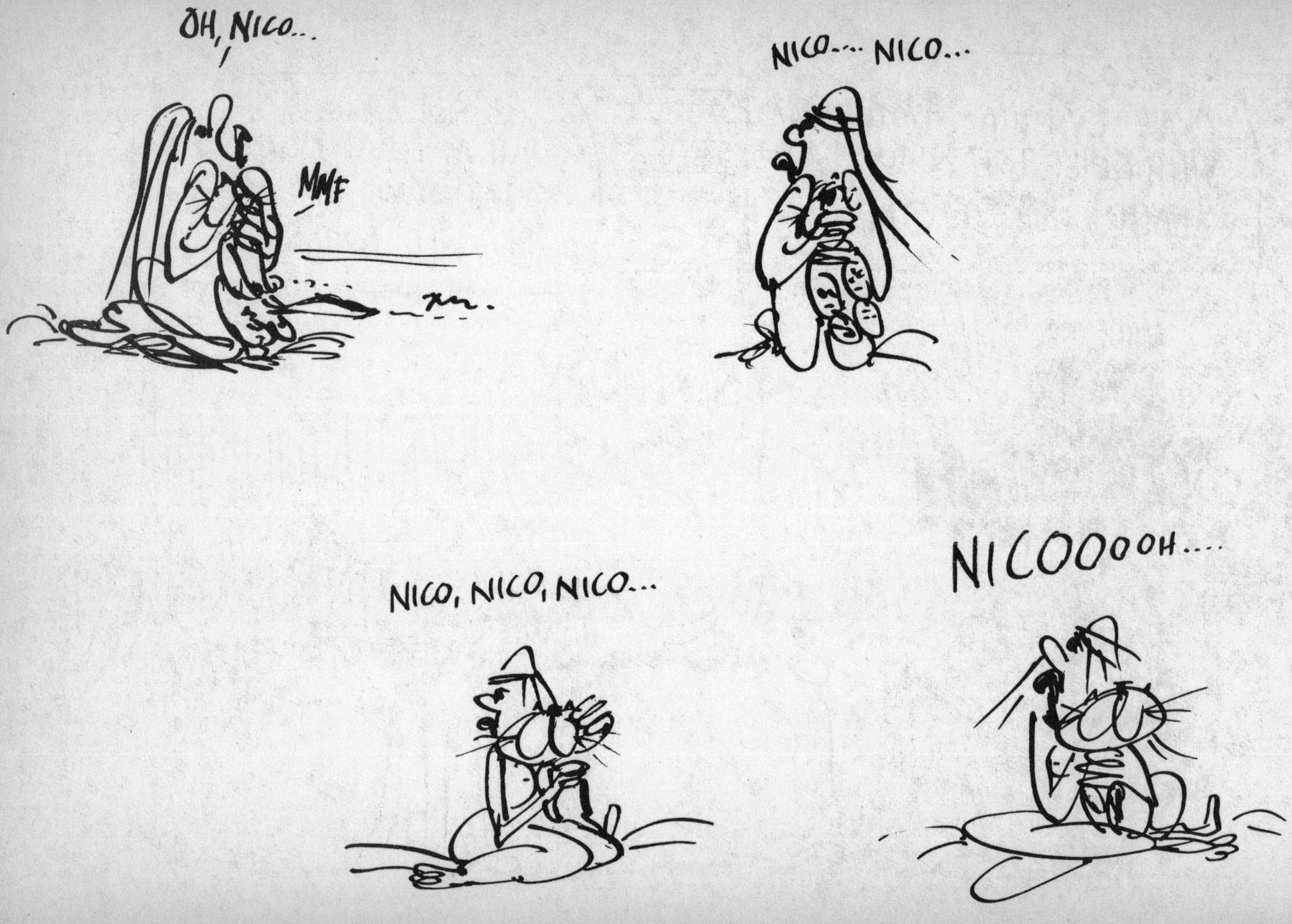
OH, NICO...
MMF
NICO.... NICO...
NICO, NICO, NICO...
NICOOOOOH....

NICO....

NICO...

NICO....

NEEEE-CO

NICO!

ARGH!

NICO NICO NICO NICO NICO
NICO NICO NICO NICO NICO

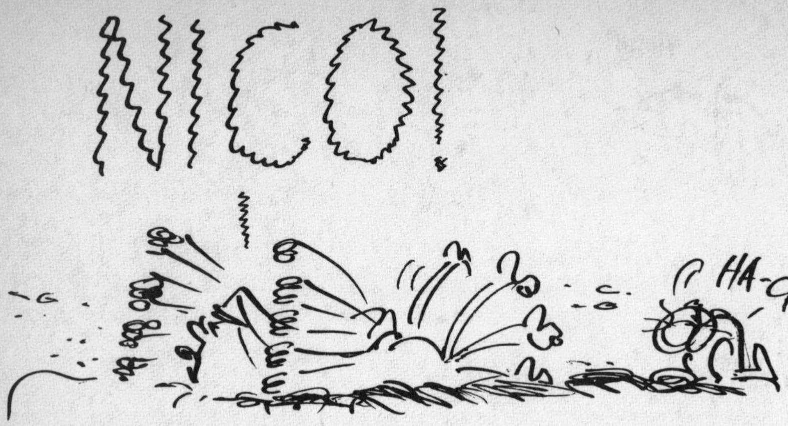
NICO!
HA-CHOO!

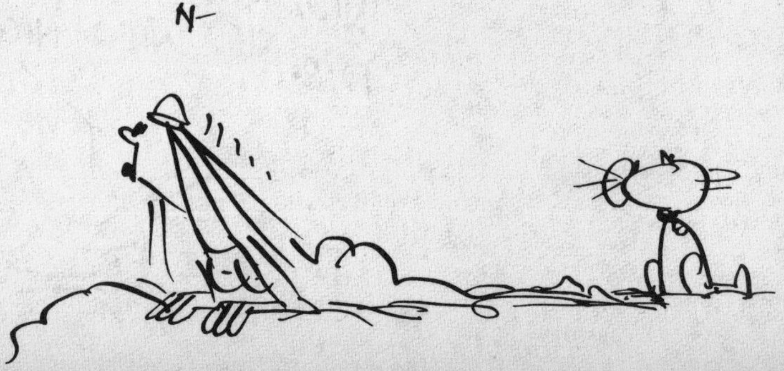
N-

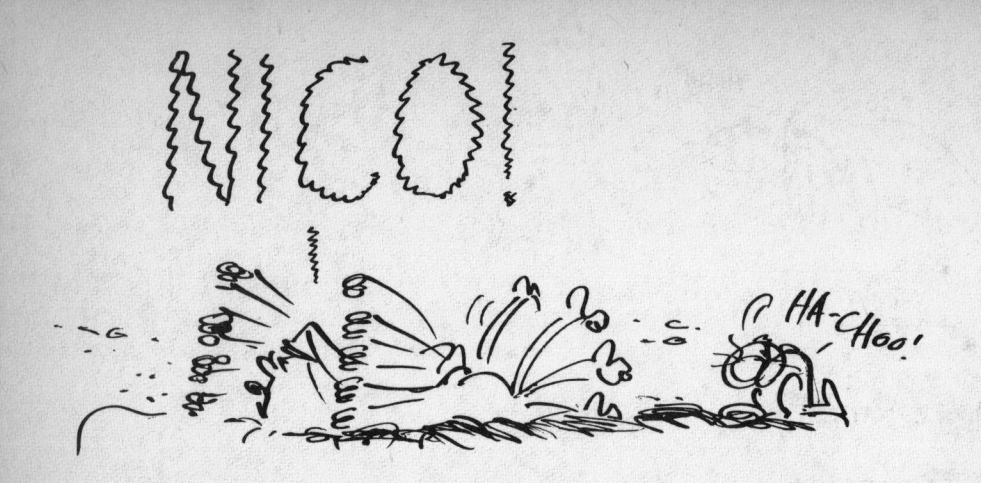

N-N-N-

N-N-N....

N-N-N-N-...

NICO!

WHUMP

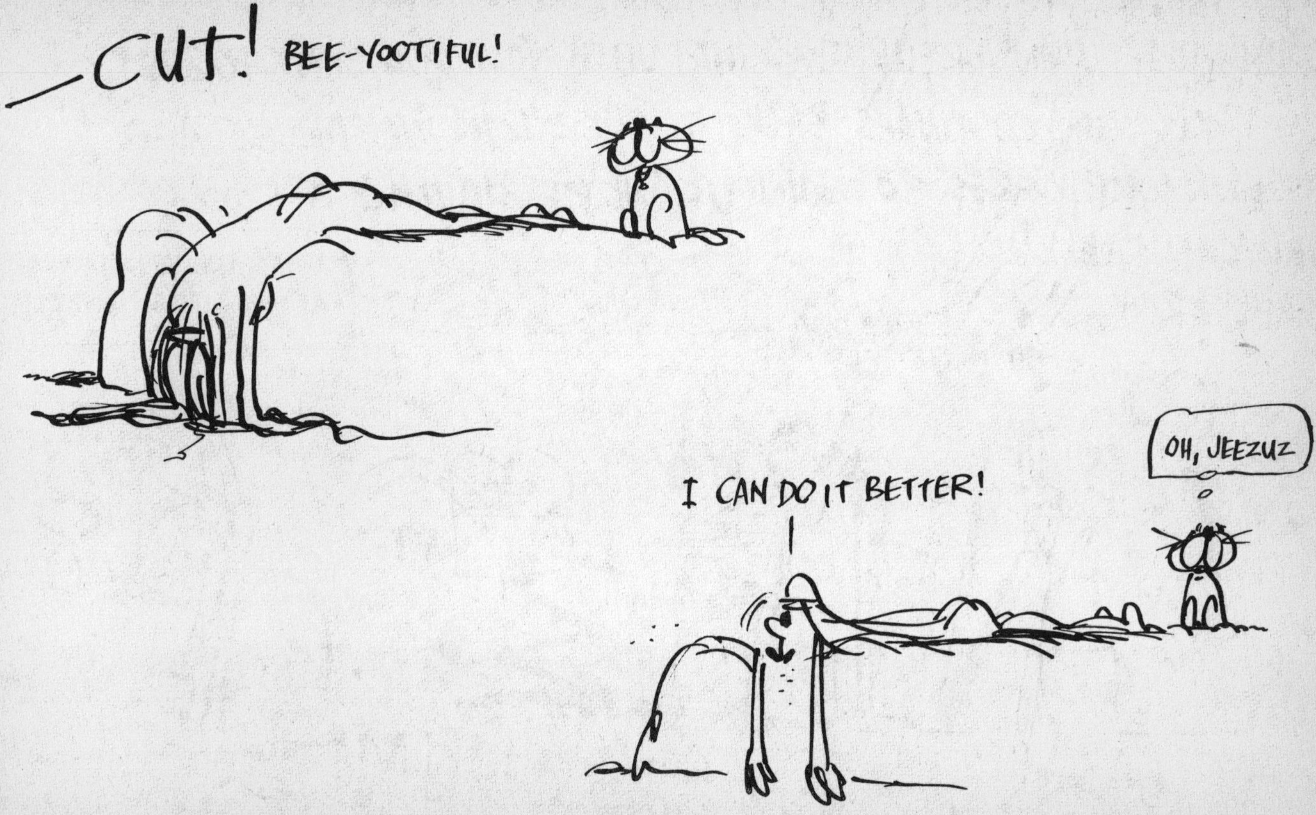
CUT! BEE-YOOTIFUL!
I CAN DO IT BETTER!
OH, JEEZUZ

OKAY-THANK-YOU-VERY-MUCH-EVERYBODY LET'S WRAP IT UP IT'S BEEN JUST WUNNERFUL WORKING WITH YOU ALL DON'T FORGET TO TAKE YOUR COSTUMES BACK TO CHERYL IN WARDROBE AND IF ENNYONE CARES TO JOIN US WE'RE HAVING A LIDDLE DRINK IN THE CAFETERIA.....

WHAT ARE YOU STARING AT YOU LITTLE PERVERT?

WOW! HEY, ROZ! THE QUEUE TO SEE BOGART'S FILM GOES HALF A MILE UP THE STREET!
WOW! HOW MANY PEOPLE ARE THERE?
ER...WELL, SEE FOR YOURSELF.
THE SEVEN SINS OF CYNTHIA
BO DINKLE
RICK PUMMEL
BOGART the CAT
BO DINKLE
BOGART THE CAT
THE SEVEN SINS OF CYNTHIA
THE SEVEN SINS OF CYNTHIA
BOX OFF
THE SEVEN SINS OF CY

TONIGHT, MY GUEST IS BO DINKLE, WHO'S LATEST FILM 'THE SEVEN SINS OF CYNTHIA' IS BREAKING BOX OFFICE RECORDS. WELCOME TO THE SHOW, BO!
THAT RHYMES!
THE BOB FOSSIL SHOW
ER... WHAT RHYMES?
"HELLO-BO-AND-WELCOME-TO-THE-SHOW"! THAT RHYMES! TEE HEE!
HEY! SO IT DOES. HAHAHA.
THIS PROGRAMME HAS TWO MINUTES TO SHAPE UP OR I'M SWITCHING OVER TO 'FARMING HOUR'.

BO, I UNDERSTAND YOU DID THE ENTIRE FILM WITH NO CLOTHES ON.
YES, BOB. BUT I ALWAYS CARRIED MY CAT "BINKY."
WHAT'S IT LIKE HAVING A CAT AS A CO-STAR?
VERY TICKLISH! HAHA!
LISTEN, BO-BABY! IT WASN'T ALL THAT EASY FOR ME, EITHER, Y'KNOW!!

LET'S SEE WHAT THE PAPER SAYS ABOUT MY NEW FILM...

HMMM.

"BO DINKLE IN THE SEVEN SINS OF CYNTHIA IS THE STORY OF BLAH, BLAH, BLAH." **AH! HERE WE ARE!** "NEWCOMER BOGART THE CAT IN THE SUPPORTING ROLE OF 'BINKY' LITERALLY STEALS THE SHOW WITH A PERFORMANCE RICH IN PASSION AND SENSITIVITY LEAVING US HUNGRY FOR MORE."

BEEP! HONK! BEE-BEEP!! HONK! BEEP! HONK! BEEP! BEEP! BEEP!

ASTORIA — HE'S BACK — BOGART IN: DESIRE IN THE AFTERNOON — A BOGART PRODUCTION — SCREENPLAY BY BOGART C. CAT

ASTORIA — BOGART THE CAT IN DESIRE IN THE AFTERNOON (WITH MERYL STREEP, JESSICA LANGE, BO OINKLE, FAYE DUNAWAY, AND SIR LAURENCE OLIVIER.) DIRECTED BY BOGART THE CAT   MUSIC BY B. CAT

SOLD OUT

OW! WATCH IT! HEY MAC! GOT ANY TICKETS? TWO? I JUST NEED TWO!!

WOW! 'HUNGRY FOR MORE'!

HERE COMES THAT CAT AGAIN, ED.
DON'T WORRY, CHARLIE. SINCE WE GREASED THE STATUE THERE'S NO WAY HE CAN GET UP HERE.
YOU SURE, ED?
ABSOLUTELY.
FLAP FLAP FLAP FLAP FLAP
'NO WAY' YOU SAID!
FLAP FLAP
HOW'D I KNOW HE COULD POLE VAULT?

I'D GO FOR DINNER BUT WHAT IF 'CAT'MANDOO IS HIDING DOWN THERE READY TO SLASH ME TO SMITHEREENS!
HMM! I KNOW! I'LL USE THAT OLD TRICK THEY USED IN THE MOVIES....THROW A PEBBLE... AND....
FLICK
THUNK

rRR **RREOWR!**
SLASH!
GARR! FSST! SLASH
SLASH
ANGRY! ANGRY!
GARR
RREOW

"YUP. HE'S DOWN THERE."

IT'S HEALTH FOOD!
BLAGH!
BOGART
WHERE ARE YOU GOING?
DOWN TO WHERE I KNOW I CAN GET SOME DECENT FOOD.
BOGART
OH NO! NOT ANDY! NOT GOOD OL' GREASY ANDY!!
ANDY'S FISH AND
TRY ANDY'S NEW FAT-FREE, LOW-CALORIE, LESS SALTY FISH N' CHIPS!
OPEN

THE WORLD HAS GONE HEALTH FOOD CRAZY. GIVE ME SOME GOOD, HONEST JUNK!
MELISSA'S HEALTH FOODS
OPEN
JULIAN'S NATURAL FIBRE
OUVERT
!
ESPONSIBLE FOR STAINS ON CLOTHING
FAT AL'S
BURGER PALACE
IT SLIDES DOWN!
MMM! SLOPPY CON CARNE 1.00
WOW!
·GREASEBURGER (8oz. of fat) 1.20
·SUPERGREASEBURGER (16oz. of fat) 1.50
·SUPERGREASEBURGER WITH CHEESE 1.55
·PLATE OF GREASY FRENCH FRIES .75
·GREASY BACON AND EGGS WITH GREASE
·GREASE SOUP WITH CROUTONS 1.00
·FAT AL'S 'GREASEBALL SPECIAL' OF THE
·GREASY CHICKEN N' CHIPS 2.50
·BAG OF TAKE-AWAY GREASE .50
·EXTRA GREASE WITH ANY OF THE ABOVE .50
urp
WOW!

BOGART! LOOK AT YOU!! YOU'RE A MESS!!
YOU SPEND THE AFTERNOON IN FAT AL'S BURGER PALACE AND SHE EXPECTS A POWDER PUFF?
KITTY FLAP
WHERE HAVE YOU BEEN?!
LISTEN, DO US A FAVOUR, WILLYA? GO AND TELL MR. McILORY....
...THAT THE PUDDLE OF OIL UNDER HIS JAGUAR WAS ME AN' NOT HIS CRANK-CASE.
NAUGHTY CAT!

AAARGH! DEE! LOOK! UNDER THE JAG! OH, NO!!
IT... IT LOOKS LIKE A PUDDLE OF OIL, STANLEY.
UH-OH.
I GUESS I SHOULDA FOUND A DIFFERENT PLACE TO EAT THAT BURGER.
...AND I JUST HAD THE @☆*!! CLUTCH DONE LAST @☆*! WEEK!!
D-DOES THIS MEAN YOU'RE GOING TO BE IN A BAD MOOD, STANLEY?
NO IT DOESN'T MEAN I'M GOING TO BE IN A BAD MOOD, DEE! IT MEANS I'M GOING TO GET BOB AT NIFTY MOTORS ON THE @☆* PHONE!!!
PLEASE DON'T BE IN A BAD MOOD STANLEY... IT'S WEDNESDAY, AND...

HALF AN HOUR LATER:

DEE! THEY SAID IT WAS HAMBURGER GREASE!!!

HAMBURGER GREASE, STANLEY?

THAT'S RIGHT! HAMBURGER GREASE! HOW COULD THE JAG' BE LOSIN' HAMBURGER GREASE???

MAYBE IT ATE A HAMBURGER! HAHAHA!

KNOCK IT OFF, DEE! THIS IS SERIOUS, GODDAMMIT! IF SOMETH— WHAT'S THAT YOU'VE GOT?

A 'FAT AL'S' HAMBURGER BOX I FOUND LYING IN THE DRIVEWAY.

WHICH MEANS MAYBE SOMEBODY WAS EATIN' A HAMBURGER UNDER THE JAG'!!!

BUT WHO WOULD DO THAT, STANLEY? WHO? HM? WHO WOULD DO A SILLY THING LIKE—

SHUT UP, DEE! I'M THINKIN'!!!

DEE!

ERK!

THE CAT!
THE CAT, STANLEY? YOU MEAN-
I MEAN THE CAT, DEE! THE CAT SOMEHOW GOT A FAT AL'S GREASY HAMBURGER AND ATE IT UNDERNEATH THE JAG'!!
GOSH, STANLEY! MAYBE THAT'S WHY THERE'S GREASE UNDER-
AND THERE HE IS, THE LITTLE-

STANLEY, PLEASE! NOT MY BEST GARDEN GNOME! STANLEY, PL—
CAT!
WINGGGGGG
DUCK!

KRASH!

"I DON'T KNOW WHAT IT LOOKS LIKE TO MR. McILROY, BUT TO ME IT LOOKS LIKE HE HIT A POLICE CAR."

"OH, STANLEY! YOU—"

"AHEM"

'CAT' MANDOO TOLD ME IF HE EVER FOUND OUT I'D BEEN MESSIN' WITH HIS GIRLFRIEND HE'D THROW A TREE AT ME.
WELL... LAST NIGHT I MESSED WITH HER...
STOMP STOMP STOMP STOMP STOMP STOMP STOMP STOMP
AND THIS MORNING HE FOUND OUT.
RRRRIP

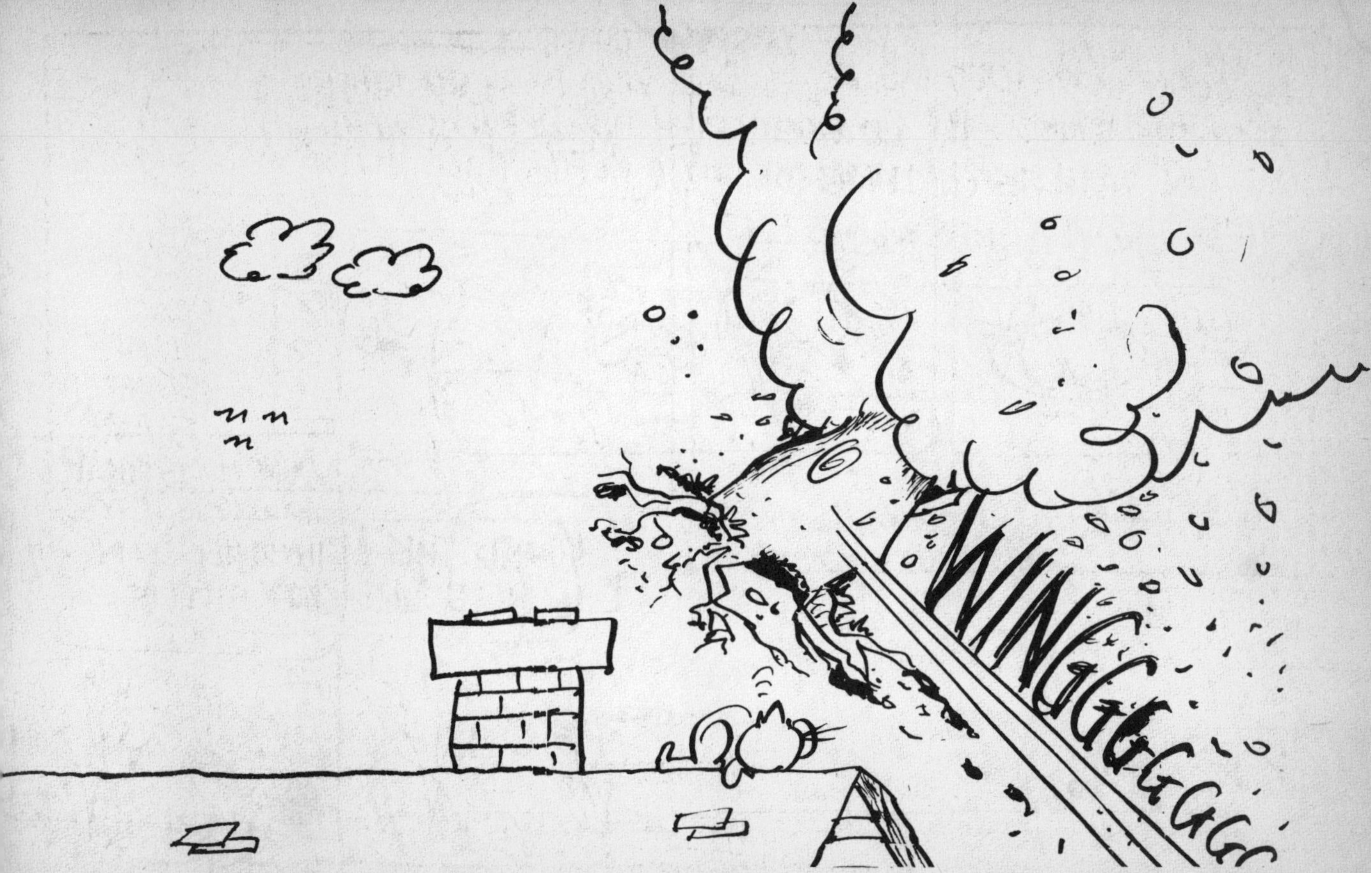
WINGGGGGGGG

QUINCY, HERE, AN' ME OUGHT TO FORM A PARTNERSHIP.
LIKE STARSKY AN' HUTCH OR DEMPSEY AN' MAKEPEACE WE'LL WORK TOGETHER TO FIGHT CRIME AND CORRUPTION AN' MAKE THE CITY A BETTER PLACE TO LIVE.
RIBBIT.
QUINCY LIKES THE IDEA AS LONG AS IT DOESN'T INVOLVE CROSSING ANY BUSY STREETS.

SOMETHING TELLS ME THAT WASN'T A VERY GOOD IDEA...
SHE DOESN'T LOOK LIKE SHE'S EVER BEEN ON ONE BEFORE AND BESIDES—
OH NO!!

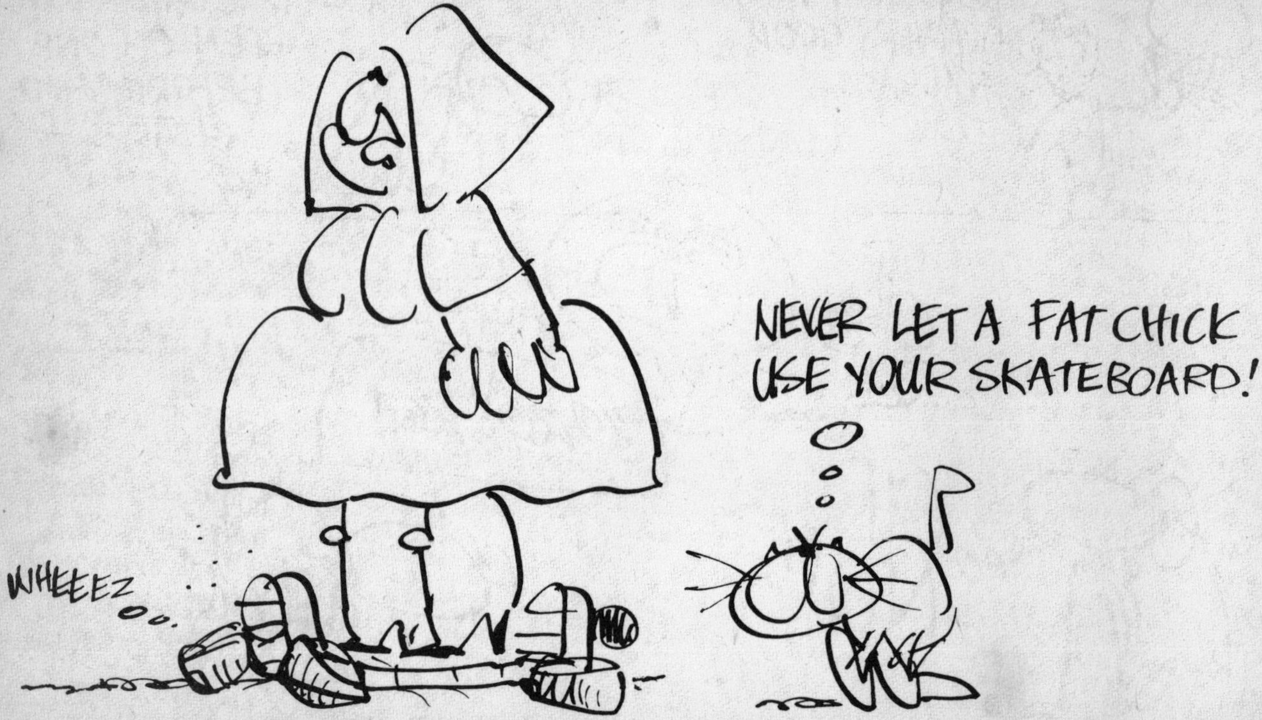
WHEEEZ
ooo
NEVER LET A FAT CHICK USE YOUR SKATEBOARD!

FOR THE SAKE OF DECENCY IN THE COMMUNITY, THERE GOES A DOG WHO COULD SURE USE A PAIR OF Y-FRONTS.

LOOK, ED! THERE'S ANOTHER PEANUT!
YEAH! AND HERE COMES THAT CAT AGAIN!!
DO YA THINK I CAN BEAT HIM TO IT?!
I DUNNO, CHARLIE, BUT YOU BETTER DECIDE QUICK!!
HERE GOES!
GO, CHARLIE!! GO! GO! GO!!!
ZAZ
WHAM!
OOOH! SO CLOSE, CHARLIE... SOOO CLOSE!
ARRGH!!